MW01120399

Out of Time

Out of Time

Peter McPhee

James Lorimer & Company Ltd., Publishers
Toronto, 2003

First publication in the United States, 2003

James Lorimer & Company Ltd. acknowledges the support of the Ontario Arts Council. We acknowledge the support of the Government of Canada through the Book Publishing Industry Development Program (BPIDP) for our publishing activities. We acknowledge the support of the Canada Council for the Arts for our publishing program. We acknowledge the support of the Government of Ontario through the Ontario Media Development Corporation's Ontario Book Initiative.

Cover Design: Clarke MacDonald

Canada Cataloguing in Publication Data

McPhee, Peter, 1957–
    Out of time

ISBN 1-55028-797-4 (bound)   ISBN 1-55028-796-6 (pbk.)

I. Title.

PS8575.P44O98 2003   jC813'.54   C2003-904205-7

James Lorimer
& Company Ltd.,
Publishers
35 Britain Street
Toronto, Ontario
M5A 1R7
www.lorimer.ca

Distributed in the United States by:
Orca Book Publishers,
P.O. Box 468
Custer, WA USA
98240-0468

Printed and bound in Canada

For Sue

Chapter 1
Jamie

Jamie sat watching the water rush from the taps, slowly filling the tub in his parents' bathroom. He had waited almost a full hour after they had gone out for the evening before taking the pills and coming up here. His heart was pounding, so he held his hands under the taps and stared at the warm water splashing over his palm, finding it relaxing and hypnotic. Or was that the pills? When the bath was full, he turned off the taps and lay back, letting the warmth rush over him, keeping his head just above the surface. He tried to will his mind to clear, to become a blank slate. For whatever reason, his first thoughts were of school.

It had been a miserable year for all of them. He, Cathy, and Sarah had spent a great deal of time together since the Christmas break, mostly talking about Sarah's latest obsession: death. It had been overwhelming, all the stats she had dug up, all the info she had given them. At first, he and Cathy had been weirded out by all of Sarah's books and videos and endless chatter on the subject, but slowly he began to see her point of view. It didn't take long for him to switch to her side; everything Sarah said made so much sense.

Sarah had a way of clearing away all the garbage, of getting to the truth. And the truth was that their lives basically sucked. There was no getting around it. And what was there to look forward to after graduation? Just more school, a boring job, a mortgage, kids, then — finally growing old and dying. He had heard this many times from his parents and he knew they were miserable most of the time. Why would his life be any better than theirs? In fact, according to Sarah's research, chances were it would only get worse for their generation. They had low-paying jobs to look forward to, costs rising, an environment completely shot — not to mention terrorists and all kinds of crazies ready to kill anyone they think is the enemy.

Yeah, what a wonderful world they'd inherit. It was filled with hate and fear; Jamie felt those things around him every day.

Sarah had told him a lot about suicide, about how society had viewed it through the ages. He knew that Christians, especially Catholics wouldn't even let a suicide be buried on holy ground. They thought that suicides went straight to hell. He didn't know what his own religion thought about the subject, and he could hardly walk up to his Rabbi and ask him.

"Funerals?" Rabbi Stern would say. "Why are you interested in that subject? When I was your age I was more interested in girls and sports and doing well in school. You've plenty of time yet to start thinking about funerals."

That was how he imagined the conversation would go, at least. He didn't know for sure because he could never get up the nerve to ask. So he did his own research and found out about the secret world of the Burial Society, of the holy men, the Chevra Kadisha, who performed the ritual washing and purification of the body. For thousands of years this society had taken care of all the details of burial. He read about the Tachrichim, the sleeveless linen burial shroud that the body was sewn into. He'd been stunned to read you could even get a kosher coffin.

He thought of his parents again, their casual comments about the old days, when they were young and only had to worry about themselves. They never knew he was listening to their conversations, even while he was playing video games or working on his computer.

Sarah had pointed out plenty of things to him over the last few months, but there were a few he'd known all along. Like the fact that he was seventeen and still a virgin; hell, he'd never even had a real date. All his life Jamie had been skinny and small, and other kids had pushed him around because of it. He had never had many real friends, not until Sarah came along. She was the first person who had accepted him, and he had fallen in love with her right from the start. Not that he could ever do anything about it, or even tell her. He knew she didn't think of him that way, and he couldn't take the chance of screwing up their friendship. Still, it would have been amazing to be more than friends. Or so he had thought. It had been more than a week since the night he and Sarah were alone in his room. He had told both Eilean and Cathy what had happened with Sarah, but neither had been much help. Eilean had just dismissed the whole thing, not in the least concerned about his feelings. He didn't blame her, really. They had hardly been close these last couple of months. Deep down he knew what Sarah had been doing, he knew the games she liked to play, the way she managed to find your deepest fear and use it against you. Jamie felt his inner calm begin to fade, knew he was getting agitated.

Relax, he told himself. There was no reason to worry anymore.

That was another thing he didn't see his future holding. If he couldn't get a girl to like him all the way through high school, what chance did he have afterwards? It was a tough world out there. He could almost see himself twenty or thirty years from now, the weird old guy that kids made fun of, who yelled at them anytime their ball acciden-tally landed in his yard. He knew they found old ladies who'd been dead for weeks, surrounded by dozens of cats and missed by no one. Did that hap-pen to old men too? Why shouldn't it?

He couldn't even imagine what he would do after school anyway. His guidance counsellor had tried to steer him into finance or insurance, since his aptitude tests said these were his strengths. He couldn't see himself spending the next forty years doing math. Jamie had no idea what he wanted to do, and in fact, he didn't want to do anything.

It seemed to Jamie that he had always been under someone else's control. At home, it was his parents; in class, it was the teachers; and in the playground, the bullies. Ron Freis and his little gang were just the latest in a series of bullies. In some ways they were the worst, because Jamie knew that at his age he should be standing up for himself, be more of a man. No matter how hard he tried, every time Ron approached him Jamie turned into the same scared five-year-old, crying at recess because someone had picked on him.

He couldn't blame his parents, not really. All his life they had tried to help him, look after him. They just didn't seem to see how hard school was on him, how lonely he had been. His mom and dad had both been popular in school and he knew that they just couldn't understand why he'd turned out the way he had. His parents had been older when they'd had him, his older brother and sister already adults with families of their own. Jamie's father joked that he'd been an "after thought." He had felt like a stranger in his family growing up. That's where Sarah had made so much sense once again. She had always known she was a disappointment to her parents, sure that life would be so much better for them, for everyone, if she could just disappear. Jamie felt the same way.

He yawned and slid under the water a little more, the surface gently lapping his ear lobes. Noticing that the water was getting cool, he wondered how long he had been sitting there. He tried to sit up to run the hot water a bit but the effort seemed too much. It wasn't that bad, really. He lifted his hands to see how wrinkled his skin was, but his eyes wouldn't focus. The pills, he thought. It's actually happening. No more worries, no more fear. Jamie smiled and felt more relaxed than he had for a long time. His limbs were getting heavier and it was harder to keep his head up — it kept tilting to the side sharply. He was proud of himself, really. Long ago he'd decided this was the best thing he could do for everyone, and now he'd worked out his whole plan, down to the last detail.

His room was clean and on his bed he had left his burial shroud of pure linen, one he and Sarah had spent hours designing and sewing. There was a note on the bathroom door telling his parents what he had done. He didn't want them just walking in here, unprepared. There had been one important thing he had learned about his faith's attitude to suicide. He knew that in Jewish tradition, the suicide was all but ignored, no one said Kadish, no one prepared the body for burial. Instead, the focus was on those left behind. Everything was done to honour the family. He liked that idea. That was how it should be. His parents should be honoured, they deserved it, just like they deserved their old lives back, and the way things were before they'd been stuck with such a hopeless son.

He thought again of Sarah, of the night last week when she had kissed him and he had been scared. It was the manic Sarah who had snuck through his window that night, the frightening Sarah. There wasn't much small talk before she got right to the point.

"You want to try something?" she asked.

"Okay," he said, a little nervously.

The kiss took him by surprise and he pushed her away. They both froze. For a moment, he thought he saw hurt in her eyes. It was gone quickly and then she grinned.

"I get it now," she said, standing up and looking at him strangely.

"Get what?" he asked, then added quickly, "You just surprised me. That's all."

She shrugged, still smiling.

"You weren't surprised," she said. "You were terrified!"

She moved closer to him. "What's the matter, Jamie? Scared of a girl?"

He tried not to, but he flinched when she reached out to him. She pushed her white-blond hair back, and he saw the brightness in her eyes, her flushed cheeks.

"All this time acting all mopey around me. Like you had such a crush on me. You deserve the Oscar, Jamie!"

"What are you talking about?" He knew what she was implying, but he couldn't think of the right thing to say. "You're all weird again," he said at last. "You're a bit creepy when you get like this."

"Creepy?" she shouted. Her face went stone cold. "*You're* calling *me* creepy?"

He implored her to be quiet, afraid his parents would hear.

"Believe me, Jamie," she said as she headed to the window. "Your parents would be relieved to find a girl in your room!"

After she left he sat on his bed wide awake, worrying. It wasn't what she thought, Jamie wanted to tell her, it was just that she scared him. Sometimes, she scared all of them. Now that it was too late, he thought of witty replies, thought of ways to explain why he had acted the way he had. It all seemed hopeless. Then he visualized himself in the future, a crazy old man alone, except for his cats.

There was no warmth left in the bathwater. From a great distance, Jamie felt himself shiver violently, but by now he was far too sleepy to care. He closed his eyes as he slipped slowly, silently beneath the water.

Chapter 2
Eilean

Little idiots.

Eilean had been stuck behind them for a few minutes, watching for an opening as they straggled slowly down the sidewalk. An ambulance screamed around the corner, siren blasting, and she nearly crashed into the girls when they stopped to watch it go by. Why were people so amazed by ambulances anyway, Eilean wondered. Because they're shiny? Because they make noise?

"Excuse me!" Eilean said, hoping they would notice her tone. As she pushed past, she saw they were a few years younger than her, probably grade eights. She walked even faster, her feet hitting the dusty pavement hard, feeling a twinge of pain with each step. She wanted to punish herself for being stupid again.

Why be mad at Sarah? she thought. Sarah only done what she always did. Drop you and then show up unexpectedly, wanting to buy your friendship back with love or presents. Whatever she thought worked better on your insecure little brain.

Since the day Eilean had met her back in the third grade Sarah had always pulled this kind of thing. She was always moody, acting for a while like your best friend, telling you every intimate detail of her life, and expressing interest in your life. Then she would become distant, hardly ever leaving her house. Since the beginning of school in the fall, Sarah's moods had become much worse. Eilean had barely seen Sarah or the others in the last few weeks.

That's why she was so surprised when Sarah arrived last night at the cramped condo Eilean shared with her father. Sarah seemed a little apprehensive, not sure what kind of reception she would receive. Eilean had been polite enough, but she wasn't ready to forgive Sarah so easily this time.

She had arrived with a full backpack and when Eilean asked what was in it, Sarah said she would tell her once they were in Eilean's bedroom. Reluctantly, Eilean led her down the hall. Sarah walked in first, quietly. Eilean lagged a bit behind, waiting. Let her make the first move, she thought.

Eilean's room was small, made even smaller by all the things she'd crammed into it — the stuffed animals, photographs, stacks of magazines, her mom's old acoustic guitar. The largest bits of furniture were the dresser that doubled as a makeup area, computer desk and the single bed, which Sarah sat on, clutching the backpack to her chest. Eilean leaned against the wall next to her dresser, keeping her distance.

"I know you must be mad at me, right?" Sarah asked. Her friendliness was a little too forced, her smile a little too wide. Eilean crossed her arms and waited. Sarah spoke in a rush.

"Of course you are. I haven't been much of a friend lately. You probably think, stupid Sarah being all moody again, right? But …"

"I don't really care anymore, Sarah," Eilean interrupted. "You've done this to me so many times." Watching Sarah sitting on the bed, that forced smile on her face, Eilean knew it was true. It wasn't just that Sarah had these mood swings — she manipulated people. All her ups and downs, her disappearing and suddenly showing up again. That's how she controlled her friends.

"I know I've ignored you. Again!" Sarah said shaking her head, a tiny smile on her lips. "But you know what a year it's been. You're the only one who knows. The only friend I trusted."

Ignore her, Eilean told herself. Don't let her play you this time. Eilean looked at the ceiling, brushing a strand of thin hair from her eye.

"Everyone at school still looks at me like I'm a freak. And that stupid Klein! Always sticking her nose into stuff that's none of her business!" She glanced over at Eilean. "Like I have to tell you that!"

Sarah was silent now. Eilean followed her gaze toward the dresser. Her monitor was there, covered with the Beanies she used to collect. There was a mirrored tray that held her cosmetics and

17

perfume — not that Eilean spent much time in front of the mirror. Taped to the dresser mirror was a photograph taken three years ago on a school trip to Banff. There were four kids in the picture standing in front of a waterfall. Eilean was on the far left, dirty blonde hair plastered to her face by the spray. Jamie was beside her, short and dark, his smile a little tentative at having Cathy's arm wrapped around his shoulder. Sarah was in the front, grinning wildly, her hair so blonde it was almost white, an overexposed blur.

Eilean looked at the picture, then back at Sarah. She hadn't noticed the changes before. Sarah had always been thin, but now she was kind of scrawny. Her cheekbones were prominent beneath the dark smudges under her eyes. Eilean had always been jealous of Sarah's skin, but now it was yellowish and blotchy. Sickly.

"I almost forgot!" Sarah blurted out. She opened the backpack and spilled the contents onto the bed. "These are for you!"

Eilean stared in disbelief as Sarah pulled out books, ones she had wanted to borrow, a video game they had been hooked on back in Junior High, CDs that Eilean had once told Sarah she really enjoyed.

"What is this?" Eilean asked, stepping a bit closer. Sarah looked up at her, and Eilean saw for the first time the effort Sarah was making to appear happy.

"Presents! Stuff I know you've always liked."

"Why?"

"Just call it an early birthday surprise."

"Early? No kidding!" It was May and Eilean's birthday was over three months away. Eilean walked closer to the bed and looked at the stuff piled there. Not bad, she began to think, some of this is pretty cool. She saw a small gold chain slithering out from under one of the CDs and hoped it wasn't what she thought it was. As she pulled it free, she saw the tiny gold unicorn hung on the chain, and she turned to glare at Sarah. It was the one Jamie had given Sarah for Christmas last year.

You bitch! she thought, suddenly angry. How could you!

"I didn't think even you were this cold," Eilean said as she dropped the unicorn back on the pile.

"I just wanted to give you some nice things. I just want us to be friends again."

"Oh, yeah?" Eilean said. She couldn't stop the anger from welling up. "Friends like in grade five, when you dumped me for weeks while you hung out with your dance class friends? Or friends like in grade eight, when you only hung out with the other cheerleaders? At least until they dumped you when you got kicked off the squad. Friends like in the last few months when you and the others pretty much shut me out?"

Sarah shook her head. "I told you, I know how lousy …"

"Save it," Eilean said. She grabbed the things Sarah had tried to bribe her with and stuffed them into the backpack.

19

"What are you doing?" Sarah asked.

"I don't want your stuff," Eilean said. "You're not buying me."

Eilean tossed the backpack to Sarah, who grabbed it in mid-air. She stared at it, holding it at arms length as if it were contaminated.

"This is wrong," she said at last. "This isn't what was supposed to happen—"

Eilean cut her off. "Is that why you're all upset? Because I didn't cave in, because good old Eilean didn't act according to plan?"

Sarah looked at her, confused, not responding.

"I just … I just wanted to be friends again. That's all."

Eilean saw that Sarah was hurt, truly hurt. She looked small, defenceless, and she seemed to be trembling slightly.

Eilean took a deep breath and stopped herself from walking over and hugging her. A voice inside her whispered: Admit it, Eilean. It's been so lonely without her.

"I'll make you a deal," Eilean said. "Meet me at the VitalBean tomorrow before class. We can talk then. Okay?"

Sarah hesitated. "Tomorrow? I don't …"

Eilean opened the door and pushed Sarah gently out of her room.

"Tomorrow at eight. We'll talk."

Sarah nodded, and they walked back downstairs.

"Listen Sarah," Eilean said as they reached the stairs. "You know how hurt Jamie'd be if he knew you tried giving the unicorn away."

"Jamie doesn't care anymore," Sarah said.

"Yeah, right!" Eilean replied. "Hold on to it. If you hurt Jamie again, I'll break your neck!" Sarah just looked at Eilean, not saying a word.

Eilean had sat for nearly a half-hour at their usual booth in the VitalBean before admitting to herself that Sarah wasn't going to show. She finished her coffee and started the walk to school, running into the giggling teens less than a block from the coffee shop.

It wasn't a very long walk from her house to school, and usually at this time of year it was rather pleasant. Her school was in the far northwest of Calgary and the walk took her through a thickly forested park, with the huge ski jump of Canada Olympic Park visible straight ahead, framed by the Rockies. This early in the morning, the mountains stood in sharp contrast to the blue sky and sunlight glistened on the snow-covered peaks.

Chief Calf Robe Secondary was on a gentle slope and her path took her to the rear of the school first. Usually at this time of the morning, the boys' football team would be practising in the field and the junior kids would be running on the track surrounding it. But that morning the field was empty. No one at the back doors. No faces at the windows. She walked on and the front of the school came into sight — along with an ambulance, police cars and several vehicles from the school board. On the wide front steps she saw Mr

21

Powers, the vice-principal, and standing next to him was Miss Klein, the school's counsellor. Even at this distance, Eilean saw that Klein was searching the crowd, looking for someone. Eilean felt a sickening lurch in the pit of her stomach. Someone jostled her. She dropped her backpack and a can of pop, part of her lunch, clattered on the cement. She always forgot to close her bag properly. Miss Klein and the vice-principal turned at the sound. They started walking toward her.

Chapter 3
Ron

Something caught Ron Freis' eye just as he was about to enter the auditorium. He thought he'd seen a quick flash of white-blond hair, a pale girl hiding in the shadows across the hall, watching him.

"Watch it, jerk!" a voice shouted. He'd stopped so suddenly that the kids behind him had crashed into each other. He turned slowly and glared down at the kid who had insulted him. The boy looked about fourteen, and as the colour drained from his pimply face, Ron saw that the boy recognised him. He felt glad that he still had a reputation, even if he knew it was fading, could feel it going.

"Did you say something?"

The kid looked up at Ron. "Sorry. I didn't mean it."

"Next time, think before you open your mouth," Fritz shouted, leaning over the boy. Ron hadn't seen Fritz approach, but suddenly he was there, viciously shoving the boy. The boy fell backwards and slammed into the lockers. The crowd parted as Fritz closed in on him. Ron grabbed Fritz by the arm.

"Leave it," Ron said.

"He dissed you! We gotta teach him a lesson."

"He got it already," Ron said.

He couldn't care less about the kid sitting on the floor, but he didn't see the point in hurting him. Fritz pulled his arm free from Ron's grip, shaking his head.

"You getting weak?" he asked, stepping close, their faces only inches apart. "Last week with that little punk in gym and now this."

"The kid's learned. Just leave it." Ron looked down at the kid.

He just sat there, frozen, eyes darting around, and Ron thought: Jesus ... I can practically see the wheels working in your little brain.

Then Fritz pushed past Ron, deliberately checking him with his shoulder. Ron waited a moment, closing his eyes, trying to ignore what Fritz had done, the disrespect he had shown. Things had been tense between them since last summer. Fritz had wanted to be with Spook, Ron knew. He never got past the fact that Ron found her first. Ron opened his eyes and saw the boy staring up at him, still sitting against the lockers, too scared to move.

A year ago, Ron wouldn't have cared what Fritz did to the kid, hell, he might even have joined in. But for some reason he felt different these days, and he couldn't understand why that was. Maybe

Spook had done it, maybe she had changed him.

Ron turned away.

It was crowded and noisy inside the auditorium, the seats filled to capacity. Those students who hadn't found a seat milled around the stage or near the exits. As he looked around, he saw four or five teachers on the stage. Three of them were women and he saw that they were crying.

Ron looked for his pals. Fritz had joined the others on the first set of seats and shouted out to them. Chucky raised a fist in the air.

"Let me get you a seat, my man," he shouted. He turned to the kid on his right and shoved him onto the floor. The kid scrambled up and slinked away. The group slid along the bench, leaving a spot for Ron. He sat beside Fritz, who gave him a sidelong glance and then ignored him.

"Whazzup?" Chucky asked, reaching across the others to give him a high five. Chucky was his oldest friend, and had lately gotten into hip-hop, even trying to pull the look together, complete with the wool cap, saggy pants, and the puffy jacket. Ron thought he looked like a clown, and had no problem saying so — every time he had a chance. Chucky didn't seem to get the sarcasm.

"Not much, Foolio," Ron replied. He nodded at the two other guys, Boomer and State. The latter two still dressed pretty much the same way they had for years, the same way Ron dressed. Their chosen uniform consisted of worn leather and ripped Levis.

"Too bad I have to miss History for this," Ron said, trying to keep it light.

"Sucks to be you," Fritz replied coolly. Ron gave him a hard look. Fritz just sat there, his expression unreadable.

"So what's this all about?" Ron asked no one in particular. Chucky pulled off his earphones and shrugged a ghetto shrug. Ron could easily make out the x-rated lyrics of the music.

"Word's that someone offed themselves."

"Must've got an extra dose of stupid," Fritz said, shaking his head.

"Yeah," State added, "like the dose you got!" He finished with a punch on his pal's shoulder. Fritz looked annoyed and he obviously didn't get the joke.

"That's a lie, man! I told you already I never had a dose of nothing!"

The others laughed at this, and Fritz just glared. Same old Fritz, Ron thought, never got a joke in his life. He wondered why he still bothered with these guys. He wondered about that a lot these days.

"It's got nothing to do with being stupid," Ron said.

"Suppose you tell us what is it then?" Fritz asked. "Since you're so much more mature than us now."

"They're just gutless," Ron said. The others nodded (with the exception of Fritz) as if this was the wisest thing they had ever heard. "My old man told me that a long time ago. It's one of the few things I agree with him on."

Ron despised his father, and it had been hell growing up in his house. He was now bigger than his old man, who hadn't gotten up the guts to raise a hand to him in a long time. The verbal attacks had just become worse.

Chucky looked toward the stage. He nodded, thinking it over. "Yeah," he said softly. "Gutless. That's what they are."

One of the teachers stepped up to the microphone and tapped it. There was a screech of feedback and most kids yelled and booed. The teacher raised his hands and called for silence. After a few moments, the room was relatively quiet.

The teacher took the microphone from its stand and stood there for a moment, as if trying to think of what he was going to say. Ron knew him, vaguely. The guy taught English or Social Studies or something. Ron had never had him in any of his classes.

"Could I ask the people near the doors to close them, please?"

They all waited while the doors were slammed shut.

"Good. Now people, I know you are wondering what is going on. No doubt there's a lot of speculation out there. I'm afraid we have some terrible news to tell you. One of the students here at Calf Robe has tried to commit suicide."

The teacher waited as the crowd erupted again.

Ron looked around at the crowd. He saw that some of the girls had burst into tears.

How pathetic, he thought. They don't even know who it was! Then he suddenly remembered the white-haired girl in the hall earlier. He turned to quickly look over his shoulder but the girl he was hoping to see wasn't there.

"The student was discovered early this morning," the teacher continued. "We are withholding the name until the police have finished their investigation and the family has been notified."

Ron glanced over at his friends, who were still shaking their heads.

"We have no word on the condition of this student at the present time, but she was rushed to hospital in serious condition. Now, we know that this is a traumatic thing for all of you. The school board will provide counsellors and they will be available for anyone who needs them. The staff and myself will also be available for anyone who needs to talk. And I want to say on behalf of the entire staff here at Chief Calf Robe, our hearts and prayers go out to the family, and we know all of you feel the same way. Now, I have another announcement, and please, remember the serious situation here." He paused a moment. "All classes have been cancelled for the day."

A few of the kids still cheered, Ron noticed, Fritz and Chucky among them.

The doors were opened and the kids began to filter out. Some hung together in clumps, hugging each other, sobbing. Some just looked stunned. Ron felt contempt for all of them. He shook his head as he and his buddies pushed their way through the crowd.

"Gutless," Ron said again, almost to himself. He had made it to the exit when a hand grabbed him by the upper arm. Ron spun around and glared down at the man who held him.

"Where do you think you're going, Freis?" The man was Mr Jenkins, head of the Sports faculty.

"You heard. All classes are cancelled."

"Not for you. You still owe me some detention time."

"Get real!" Ron shouted. "There's no school today! You can't do this!"

"Sure I can," Jenkins said. Chucky stepped between Ron and the teacher. "Hey, leave my bro be, man!"

Jenkins looked the boy up and down, shaking his head slightly at the outfit.

"Just step back, Beastie Boy, or you'll be joining your *bro*!"

Chucky stepped away from the teacher, still trying to look cool. Jenkins took Ron by the arm and led him through the crowd toward the detention hall. Chucky yelled at the teacher, trying to save face.

"Yo! It's Beastie Boys, man! And it's a group, not a person!"

Jenkins didn't bother to look back.

"Oh well," he shouted. "You're not much of a person either."

Chapter 4
Eilean

Suicide attempt. Intensive care. Tragic.

They kept on speaking to her, Mr Powers and Miss Klein, but to Eilean it was only a monotonous drone she barely heard as she sank lower in her chair, all these crazy thoughts racing through her brain. She tried to push away the image of a blonde girl hanging from the ceiling, but it kept coming back, her imagination filling in every gruesome detail.

Why did I ignore Sarah? Why did I have to be so stubborn, shut her out like that? Oh my God! Cathy and Jamie, they have to hear about Sarah. And not like this.

"… too late for Jamie."

At the mention of Jamie's name, Eilean looked up at Mr Powers.

"What did you say?"

Mr Powers looked at Miss Klein. He ran a hand through his hair and took a deep breath.

He's shaking, she thought. What now? Eilean crossed her arms protectively.

"There's more bad news. I know Jamie Seilig was a friend of yours …"

He kept on speaking but she focused on that one word, *was*. Jamie was … Was! That was all her mind could register. Nothing else made it through the walls that rose up around her. *Jamie was!* Then someone screamed and it sounded like it came from a long way off. She heard sobbing, a chair overturning.

Jamie's dead!

Someone called Eilean's name. Slowly she became aware that hands were holding her, lifting her. She looked around as the world rushed back at her.

"Eilean," Miss Klein was saying, leaning over her. "Please, calm down."

Mr Powers took Eilean by the arms and helped her to her feet, holding her steady. She saw his assistant standing behind him, hands covering her mouth, tears on her pale face. On the wall behind her, there was a long row of trophy cases.

That's wrong, Eilean thought, blinking. Those are supposed to be in the hallway. She looked around her and realized they were outside the admin offices. Except for a small group of staff surrounding them, the hallway was empty. A security guard stood nearby. The clock above him read 9:22.

"It's okay, Eilean," Mr Powers said as he led her back to his office. "Please step back," he called out

31

to the others. Inside, he lifted the chair that had been upturned and sat her gently down. He poured a glass of water and held it out for her. She stared at it.

"Please," he said. "Take a sip."

Eilean took the glass from his hands, not really wanting it. She shook so badly that the water spilled over her hands and the front of her shirt. Mr Powers took the glass away.

"We should take her to the nurse," he told Miss Klein.

"I don't want the nurse! I need to find Cathy."

Mr Powers and Miss Klein exchanged glances. Eilean sat up, her heart pounding. "What? What about Cathy?"

"We tried to find her this morning," Miss Klein said. "When we called her mother, she told us Cathy left early for school. And you haven't seen her either?"

Eilean shook her head.

"Have you any idea where she might go?" Mr Powers asked.

She shook her head again, staring at the floor. The image came back of a girl hanging in Klein's office, except this time, instead of the pale blonde, she pictured a small, dark-haired girl. Cathy.

"It's important that we find her as soon as possible," Miss Klein said. Eilean looked up.

"Why the rush?"

"We want to make sure Cathy's okay," Miss Klein said.

"Like you made sure Sarah was okay?" Eilean said, glaring at her. It was easy to be angry with Klein.

"My concern has always been the welfare of my students," Miss Klein said.

"Then how the hell do you keep your job?" Eilean replied.

"Enough!" Mr Powers said. "This won't help."

"Maybe you just missed her in the crowd or something."

"We're sure she isn't at school," Miss Klein said. Eilean ignored her, speaking only to Mr Powers.

"I know some places she likes to hang out. I can go look for her."

Mr Powers walked behind his desk and sat heavily in his chair. He glanced at some notes and Eilean waited, heart pounding. What weren't they telling her?

"It seems when these, these incidents occur," he began, "and more than one child's involved ..." Mr Powers' voice trailed off. Eilean waited, staring at him until he began again.

"There may be a pattern emerging." He nodded to Miss Klein.

"We've found that more than one act," Miss Klein stopped, seeming to collect her thoughts. She began again. "More than one attempt indicates a pact."

"A pact?" Eilean asked. For a moment the word had no meaning.

"What Miss Klein is saying," Mr Powers said, "is that friends plan this together."

"That's just whacked!" Eilean said. "I can't believe they sat around planning to kill themselves!" She felt tears about to flow again. Sure they talked about death, over and over again until she got sick of it. Sick of them. But it was all just talk! She would have known if they were serious.

Wouldn't she?

Mr Powers leaned forward, elbows on his desk, hands clasped together. "Eilean. We didn't bring you here just to tell you about your friends. We brought you here to protect you."

Eilean's head snapped toward him. "Protect me from what?"

"When I found Sar ..." Miss Klein stopped and closed her eyes. She took a deep breath before continuing. "After this morning, we're sure there's a pact. We think you're part of it."

"Do I look dead to you?" Eilean said, a look of disbelief on her face. "Would I bother coming to school if I was about to kill myself?" Then the thought occurred to her: That's exactly what Sarah did.

"As a matter of fact, of all the group," Miss Klein said in that crisp voice of hers, "After looking through your school record, I consider you the most likely candidate."

"Oh, really?" Eilean said. "And how did you come up with that brilliant theory?"

"To start, there's your mother's history ..."

Eilean shot forward in her chair.

"My mother! Jesus! What are you talking about?

My mother's been dead for, like, thirteen years!"

"You know it's an important factor," Miss Klein said.

Eilean subsided a little and just shook her head. She hated to admit it, but they were right. Mr Powers spoke again.

"We've contacted your father," he said.

"He's not in the city."

"He's taking the next flight down. He should be here by mid-afternoon."

Eilean felt the fear return. "Why is my father flying here? What did you say to him?"

"We told him what we told you. He agreed with us and wanted to come home right away."

Eilean stood and began to pace the small area near the closed door of the office. Mr Powers also stood, almost as if afraid Eilean would run out the door. "Don't worry," Mr Powers said. "He knows you're with us. That you're safe."

"And that makes it better? He still thinks I'm in some stupid suicide pact! Do you know what that'll do to him? After what my mother did?"

"Eilean, we know you're upset ..." said Miss Klein.

"Upset?" Eilean yelled, walking over to Miss Klein, leaning over her. "I'm past upset! I'm pissed! About this school not having a clue about what's happening here every day! About this stupid meeting and your stupid theories. About how you had to go and freak out my dad!"

Miss Klein sat very still.

"And then you bring up my mother! Don't you know that's the exact reason I'd never do something like this? Don't you think I know what it would do to my dad?"

There was a pause as the two adults waited for her to finish. She turned away, burying her head in her hands.

"We still have to find Cathy," Mr Powers said.

"I don't buy Klein's theory. Not with Cathy. She's about the sanest person I know."

"Then let's find her. Prove our theory wrong," Mr Powers said.

"Alright. Like I said, let me go find her for you."

"You can't," Mr Powers said. "The police need to talk to you first."

"So? I can be back in no time."

"There has to be a parent present when the police interview you. And until your father arrives, we can't let you leave school property."

"What do you mean I can't leave?"

"It's for your own protection—" Miss Klein began. Eilean cut her off.

"Screw you, Klein!" Eilean shouted. "You 'protected' Sarah, and look where she ended up — in your office!"

"That's enough, Eilean!" Mr Powers barked.

"I just want to find Cathy! And then we'll go to the hospital to see Sarah!"

"That's not possible," Mr Powers replied. His tone was gentle again. "Remember, Sarah's in intensive care. It'll be a while before she can have visitors." He stood and came around the desk, sitting on the edge. "Look. You're in shock. We all are. There are counsellors coming, and I think you should talk to one of them."

"I don't need to talk," Eilean said, shaking her head.

"I'll tell you what," Mr Powers said. "You need to take a moment to absorb everything. Would you like some time alone? You can stay here in my office, or we can take you to a classroom."

Eilean didn't like either idea, and yet she knew she needed to be alone. "A classroom," Eilean said. "Please."

"Alright then. I'll call down to Mr Robertson's classroom. Miss Klein, please see she gets there safely, and then we should join Principal Stuart and the police."

Miss Klein escorted Eilean from the office, gripping her arm as they walked through the empty halls. Mr Powers had tried to be kind, but now Eilean felt like a prisoner again.

Chapter 5
Eilean

Eilean pulled her arm free from Miss Klein's grasp. "So," Eilean asked, trying to sound casual. "You were the first to see Sarah?"

Miss Klein looked straight ahead. "I don't think it will do any good to talk about this right now."

She blinked, Eilean saw, then the tears slid down Miss Klein's cheeks. Her mouth moved, as though she was about to say something, but she just wiped the tears away and kept walking. They stopped in front of a classroom. "Please keep an eye on her," Miss Klein said to the teacher standing in the doorway. "I'll ... I'll check in later."

Eilean watched as Miss Klein rushed down the hall. She had never seen any emotion from the guidance counsellor in all the years she had known her.

Mr Robertson was a short, bald, round man. She'd had him for homeroom in junior high and liked him. He stepped toward her and for a moment, she thought he was about to hug her, but he seemed unsure.

"Eilean," Mr Robertson said, placing a hand on arm. "Is this where you want to be?"

She nodded.

"I can't imagine how you feel right now," he said as he led her to a desk in the front of the room. He gave her a book he'd been holding in his hand. "Here. This will keep your mind occupied until your father gets here."

She took the book and smiled at him, grateful. Robertson walked to his own desk, popped open a soda and started marking papers.

"Are you going to stay here?" she asked him.

"Well …" he hesitated. "I have to. This is the detention hall."

"Detention!"

"You're not in trouble, Eilean. It's just that someone needs to be with you right now. You can go back to Mr Powers' office if this doesn't feel right."

Eilean shook her head. She looked down at the book, and saw it was a collection of poems by Margaret Atwood. She had found the same book in her mother's things, years ago. She leafed through it, then put it down on the desk.

Eilean thought of the conversation in Powers' office.

She should have behaved better. Powers was just trying to help. But Klein deserved everything she got. Eilean decided she should have said more.

She sat up, feeling herself tense again. Thinking of Klein made her think of Sarah, and then of Jamie. She covered her eyes, feeling a catch in her throat.

She was on the verge of crying, and she fought it.

She heard the door open and took her hands away from her eyes to see something that made this ridiculous situation even more ridiculous. Mr Jenkins was dragging a very pissed-looking Ron Freis into the room. Robertson stood as they entered.

"Mr Freis, what a surprise. It's been almost a week since you last visited."

Ron ignored his comment and stared past him at the blackboard.

"He's got a little more time to put in," Jenkins said. "Maybe he'll think next time before mouthing off in my class."

"I doubt it," Robertson replied, looking directly at Ron. "Mr Freis here prides himself on acting the troubled, moody type. Don't you?" Ron just looked at the board.

"Can you keep him here until noon? Or were you leaving early to help counsel students?"

"No, I don't mind staying. I think we have plenty of help there."

Before he left, Jenkins caught Eilean's eye, offering a small smile that suggested he was both relieved and sad to see her there.

"So! I see you haven't brought any books once again, Mr Freis."

Ron's face was flushed with anger.

"It just so happens I have the perfect assignment for you right here." Robertson reached across his desk to grab a book from a stash he kept there. Eilean had a front-row view of the faded seat of his suit pants as he bent forward. He straightened up, holding a thick textbook out to Ron.

"I seem to remember that you were rather weak in algebra last year. This is the perfect time to catch up." He picked up a pad of paper and a pen and handed everything to Ron. "I want the assignment at the end of chapter ten done before you leave today."

Ron said nothing as he took the items and sat at the bench Robertson indicated. He glanced at Eilean, and for a moment, he looked a little confused at seeing her in detention. He was too angry to speak and threw his book on the bench. Robertson didn't react, but simply sat down behind his desk and started sipping his generic cola again. He bent over his papers, ignoring his detainees.

After a few moments, Eilean sneaked a glance at Ron. He sat there unmoving, arms folded and staring straight ahead. She couldn't remember ever seeing him this close before, and she had never seen him alone, without his little gang. It was funny, everyone at the school knew Ron Freis by sight, but she could count on one hand the people she knew who had actually ever spoken to him. Jamie had of course, but none of those conversations had been pleasant, or voluntary. Ron and his buddies had picked on poor Jamie practically from the first day of junior high. Those types seemed to smell a victim.

Eilean felt another wave of sorrow rise, thinking of Jamie. She lay her head down on the desk, hiding her face, fighting the tears once again. Jamie was dead and Sarah just hanging on. Was Powers right, could her friends have actually made some kind of pact?

"Head up, Eilean!" she heard Robertson say. The habit of years of running detention came through in his voice. She lifted her head and looked at him. "Just try reading it." He nodded at the book lying on the bench and his voice softened. "It'll keep your mind occupied until your dad gets here."

Eilean almost told him how he could occupy himself, but she held her tongue. He only knew one way to behave. He was at least trying to be kind.

"Can I open a window?" she asked. "I need to get some fresh air."

"Very well. But then right back to the book. Okay?"

Eilean stood and walked over to the windows. As she passed Ron, she saw he was smiling up at her. She ignored him as she opened the window, closing her eyes as she breathed in the fresh air. Another flash of Jamie dead, Sarah dying interrupted her moment of peace. She sat back down at her desk, not bothering to glance at the unopened book Robertson had given her.

The clock said 9:50 and she could hear kids shouting outside, hear birdsong. The clock hands didn't move. She opened the book of poems again and read the identification label stamped inside. Some of the signatures there went back to 1985. She looked at the clock again and was sure it still hadn't moved. There was a scraping of a chair on tile and

Eilean looked up to see Robertson stand, tipping back his drink to get the last drops. He placed the can on the desk and looked at his prisoners.

"I am going to take a small break. I want you two to behave while I'm gone. Most importantly, do not leave this room. Understand?"

Neither of them bothered to respond and after a beat, Robertson left. Ron immediately stood and began to stretch and yawn noisily. Eilean tried her best to pretend he wasn't there.

"Pee break," Ron said. Eilean looked back at him and saw he was at the outside windows, looking down at the school grounds. He continued speaking, even though she had yet to acknowledge his presence.

"He puts away at least six of those a day," Ron said, nodding at the cola can. "No wonder he's a pudgy little zit-faced freak."

Eilean still didn't speak. Like most kids at Calf Robe, she saw Ron Freis as a source of interest and fear. Most boys feared him, most girls thought he was a bullying jerk. Of course there were a few who had crushes on him. Eilean had never understood the whole bad boy appeal.

"He'll be gone at least fifteen minutes. Happens every time. Like clockwork."

Eilean picked idly at the cover of her book.

"You can talk, can't you?"

"Are you going to beat me up if I don't?"

He grinned. "You could at least nod. Or didn't your mother teach you any manners?"

"If you want to talk to someone so bad, Klein's available."

Ron shook his head and looked disgusted. "Klein!" he said, and then swore. She looked at him, surprised at his reaction to Klein's name.

"You don't like her?"

"She's a hack. She shouldn't be allowed within five miles of a school!"

"What'd she do to you?"

"It wasn't me. It was a friend she screwed over."

"What's the matter, he get some anger management lectures? Told to stop stealing the grade sevens' lunch money?"

He was silent for a moment, about to say something. She noticed that his eyes were dark, almost black, and he was genuinely angry. She saw him change his mind and look away. "Something like that."

He stood staring out the window. "You've got some mouth, for someone afraid I'll beat her up."

"I don't care what happens."

She felt a rush of emotion again, caught a glimpse of Sarah, a memory of her laughing. She bit her tongue, trying to push the image away.

"You hear what happened today?" Ron said, still looking outside.

Eilean didn't want to discuss any of this yet, and she definitely didn't want to discuss it with Ron Freis. He seemed to take her silence as a reason to keep talking.

"Some chick tried to kill herself. Can you believe

that?" His expression was a mixture of anger and disgust.

"You ever think it might have been an accident?" Eilean asked, immediately regretting it. She didn't know why she was even looking at him, let alone talking to him.

"There's no such thing as accidents!" he responded.

"What are you talking about?"

"It's like my old man says, everyone's a screw-up. And anyone who blames stuff on accidents is just a screw-up with an excuse."

Eilean shook her head. "Your dad sounds like a wonderful human being."

Ron shook his head. "Wrong. He's a lawyer."

He grinned and she assumed he had tried to make a joke. When she didn't respond, he carried on. "I'll bet it's one of those little pathetic creeps who think life is too hard."

"You've got it all figured out, right?" Eilean said.

"I know enough. I know that you have to be totally selfish to off yourself. Too weak to face the real world."

"I forgot: you're an expert on weakness, aren't you? Picking on people like Jamie!"

Eilean turned away from him, looking at the clock again. She wanted Robertson to return so she didn't have to listen to Freis anymore. She wanted her father to arrive; she wanted to get out of there. And she didn't want to think of Jamie.

"Just so you know," he said, "I never touched Seilig. It was some of my buddies that shoved him around."

"You just watched them, right? Does that make you different?"

Ron's back went rigid. He made a fist and his knuckles cracked. She decided to keep her mouth shut. It seemed pretty stupid, tormenting a bully when you were alone in a classroom with him. He looked away from her, out the window again. Eilean sat in her chair, trying to calm herself, staring at the clock. It had been less than ten minutes since Robertson had left. Then she thought of something Ron had said, that the teachers had said it was a girl who had tried to kill herself.

"Did the teachers say who this girl was?"

Ron didn't respond, didn't even move. He continued staring out the window.

"Excuse me," she said, annoyed. "I asked you something."

Ron walked back to the bench and sat down, pulling a silver cigarette lighter from the inside pocket of his leather jacket. He flipped the top and started to flick the flame on and off, on and off.

"They didn't say. I don't think they even meant to tell us it was a girl."

Eilean only nodded.

After a moment he leaned forward, his elbow on the desk.

"You know who it is, don't you?"

She ignored him. He dragged his chair across

the floor, closer to her, and she thought he looked almost concerned.

"Was she a friend of yours?"

"Why would you ask that?"

"Well, why are you here today? I'll bet you never had detention in your life."

She found herself pretending to look through the poetry book.

"Why's your dad picking you up?"

She slammed the book down. "Why is it any of your business?"

She felt the tears come and this time she couldn't hold them back. She stood up and turned away from him, sobbing, not caring anymore what he or anyone else thought. She had held it inside too long and the pain exploded from her.

"Alright, if you have to know," she shouted, her breath catching. "It was a friend! Her name was Sarah! Sarah Spokes! Are you happy now?" There was no way she would even mention Jamie as well.

She turned away and grabbed her bag, then ran to the open the door and rushed outside. She had no idea where she was going; she only knew she had to get away from him, from this school. She had to get outside to sunlight and fresh air.

She threw her bag over her shoulder and held it down with her left hand as she began to run. Somewhere behind her, she heard Robertson's voice, yelling at her to stop, to get back into the detention hall.

She ran faster.

Chapter 6
Cathy

Cathy felt a slight chill and pulled her fleece jacket tight around her. She became aware of people walking past her, some carrying drinks or ice cream. She saw that most of them were elderly and Asian, and they scowled at her as they walked past.

Am I doing something wrong, she wondered? Why do they look so mad?

Cathy looked around; it took a great deal of concentration to do even this simple task. She was just outside a snack bar in a densely forested area. Across from her was a huge parking lot with only a few cars and a tour bus parked in it. Mountain peaks surrounded them.

Tourists. They're tourists and I'm somewhere in the mountains.

Cathy looked down and saw that her backpack was sitting open on the bench beside her, taking up any space left.

Maybe that's why they were mad. She was taking

up the whole bench. How long had she been sitting there? What was she thinking about? She remembered thinking about something terribly important, but it was gone now.

Cathy remembered borrowing her mother's car, driving out of the city.

After a few moments, she remembered that morning waiting until her mother had started her shower. She remembered sneaking out of the house fully dressed, right down to her hiking boots, and slipping into the garage. It had still been dark, the sky just beginning to lighten. She had started the car with the garage door still shut.

The exhaust started filling the garage. It happened so fast. All she had to do was lie down on the seats. It would have been so simple to stay there until she fell asleep.

But then the fumes filled the car and she began to cough, gagging on them. She sat up, tears streaming as she fumbled for the remote on the car's visor. It took a few moments for the door to open and clear away the exhaust. It took a little longer for her to breathe properly, for her eyes to stop watering.

She almost smiled at the memory. Imagine not being able to kill yourself because the smell made you sick.

That was a while ago, two, maybe three hours? How long did it take to drive up to Banff? She shook her head, unable to remember.

Cathy took a deep breath and caught the sharp tang of pine, the scent of water coursing over rock somewhere nearby.

She knew where she was now.

She glanced back down at the backpack and the few items it held. Sticking out of the top was her sketchbook from art class. She had come up here dozens of times to sketch the area, the falls in particular. It was easily her favourite spot in all of Banff.

She must have zoned out again. She slowly became aware that the elderly people were moving, following their tour guide up the trail. Cathy felt a twinge of panic.

She had to get going. She had to get up there ahead of them.

She grabbed her backpack and jumped to her feet, beginning her long hike up the steep path to the upper falls of Chinaman's Gorge.

Why had she sat there like that? It was stupid. She was supposed to get there first, before any of the tourists.

There was nothing she could do about it now. Cathy was sure that most of them would stop at the lower falls. The climb was just too steep for this group. As she walked, she noticed a few of them give her a disapproving look for rushing past them. Normally she would have slowed and waited until they reached a wide part of the trail to pass them. Today wasn't a normal day and they were just in her way.

Out of my way you bunch of grave-nudgers!

She smiled, remembering that was what Sarah

called old people. It had sounded a bit harsh the first time she'd heard it, but she had gotten used to it, along with most of Sarah's other peculiar habits.

Maybe that's what we should have called ourselves. It suits us. Considering what we planned.

She had first come here on a school trip in grade eight, her first year at Chief Calf Robe, after moving from the southeast of the city. She had been slow making friends. Other Asian girls had approached her at first, but for one reason or another no real friendships had formed. It wasn't until late in November, after she had decided to take an extra art class, that she had met Sarah. She had never made a friend like Sarah before, and they were complete opposites. Sarah was slim, blonde, and outgoing, a good student. Cathy had no claim to any of that. All her life she had fought her weight, had struggled for good grades. Her mother had always pushed her to do better in school and kept her on strict diets. It was as though her mother couldn't be happy with the daughter she had.

She remembered the small plastic bowls filled with plain rice and fish that her mother packed in her lunch each day, along with the chopsticks her mother insisted she use (and reuse). Cathy had watched other kids laughing and kidding around between bites of their peanut butter and jelly sandwiches, their baloney and cheese, endless bags of chips and cans of soft drinks. She had kept to her own little corner, far away from the others.

Sarah had changed that. She brought Cathy into

her little circle along with Eilean and Jamie Seilig. Jamie was the first boy she had ever had a crush on, although she had never let anyone know. Sarah forced her to do things, go for walks and bike rides up to Nose Hill Park. For the first time Cathy felt accepted, eventually she even felt comfortable enough to eat her lunch with them. Instead of laughing at her meals, Sarah had wanted try them, thinking they were exotic. Cathy had never felt exotic before. Whether it was the change in her lifestyle, or her body just changing naturally, Cathy lost the weight. But she still had a lingering fear that it would happen again, that one day she would wake up and be the sad, fat girl once again. It didn't help that her mother still obsessed over her.

Things had been great, the four of them constantly together, sharing secrets, just hanging around. Sarah was clearly the leader of the group and had an endless supply of ideas for them. That is, when she had the time. Back then, Sarah was so popular, hanging out with a lot of different groups. That made it even more cool that she found time to spend with Cathy.

The first visit to Chinaman's Gorge had been that spring, and for Cathy it was love at first sight. At that time, there had been a petition going around to change the name of the gorge since many people found it racist. It had all been rather silly, putting a PC twist to a mountain gorge named over a century before. It was then that she had found out her own family's connection to Chinaman's Gorge. According to her grandmother, the gorge had been named in honour of one of her ancestors. Her great, great, something-or-other grandfather had been brought to Canada along with all the male members of his village to work building the Canadian Pacific railway. Many of them died, and many more stayed in Canada and started lives here. Cathy was almost amused when some moron called her an immigrant, or worse — she knew that her family had been in the west longer than just about anyone else.

Cathy stopped for a moment, leaning against the cool rock of the canyon wall towering over the trail.

I miss you grandma. Every single day.

Since she was a little girl, she and her grandmother had made monthly visits to the Chinese graveyard off McLeod Avenue. Before she was born, the city had expanded the freeway right through the middle of the Chinese section, moving dozens of graves in the process. Her grandmother said that that made it even more important to make sure the dead were honoured. They shouldn't have been disturbed like that. So she learned to honour her ancestors by lighting incense and small fires, throwing "hell bank notes" into the flames. The notes were tiny bits of paper, fake money they bought in Chinatown. Cathy remembered the scent of flowers, the stink of burning paper, and her grandmother's perfume, all mixing together on a hillside overlooking the graves.

"This is important," her grandmother said. "It will help our ancestors in the next life. If we take care of the dead, they will watch over us, protect us." Cathy never really believed it, but she went along with it anyway, mostly to spend time with her grandmother, and to hear her stories. As Cathy got older, she began to suspect that her grandmother did it for the same reasons.

Grandmother was the only person in the family who treated Cathy like a person. Cathy had spent as much time with her as she could, particularly this past summer, when she fell ill. Her grandmother had died the previous July.

Cathy felt a catch in her throat. She heard voices below and started hiking again.

She remembered her grandmother laughing when told about the plan to change the name of the gorge.

The school had joined the movement to come up with a new name for Chinaman's Gorge, and all the students were invited to come up with their own ideas. Cathy's was "Non-Caucasian Person's Descent." As usual, Sarah's was the smartest. She had studied the kind of people who usually had a mountain or other natural feature named after them and had come up with "Rich Old White Guy's Gorge." Not surprisingly, their teacher didn't submit their ideas. Not long after, the whole thing faded away. Nearly two years later, it was still Chinaman's Gorge, which was fine by her.

They had a lot of fun those first months together, and Cathy had never felt so accepted, so secure. Then, sometime between the end of grade nine and the beginning of grade ten, Sarah started to have strange mood swings. Most of the time she was the same old Sarah, bright and happy and full of energy, then suddenly she'd change. She looked tired and sick, not showing up at school for days at a time. She quit most of the activities she joined, or was thrown out.

Even her up moods became creepy; she seemed too intense, too eager to have fun. Sarah had always had a sharp tongue and easily found other people's weak spots. More than once she had hurt others with her sharp wit. But it only ever happened when she was in one of these moods. Cathy and the other two started to back away a little, seeing less and less of each other. It didn't help that on top of all this Cathy had to watch helplessly as her grandmother slowly faded away. She had needed Sarah to be there for her more than ever last summer.

None of them had seen much of Sarah then, and there was constant speculation about who she was hanging out with. Jamie said he saw her driving in a car with Ron Freis and his gang. Both she and Eilean had found the idea of Sarah hanging out with that crowd impossible to believe. When school began in September it took weeks before the old Sarah finally re-emerged. Then something terrible happened. Sarah was caught with drugs at school and somehow ended up in hospital. Cathy never found out why and she hadn't been allowed to visit. Only Eilean knew what had really happened and she refused to say anything on the subject. All kinds of rumours flew around the school, most of them ridiculous. Sarah returned to school after a few weeks, looking paler than ever. Slowly, the little gang began to assemble again and Sarah seemed almost normal. But there was something in her eyes after that, something terribly sad.

The other change in Sarah was a new obsession with death.

"Look at this," she said one morning. Eilean and Cathy were standing in line in the lunchroom, Jamie waiting for them, already holding his lunch tray. Sarah had that same look in her eye, the one that told them she was on her "up" phase. She seemed terribly excited about something and held out a book. "I've been reading this and it's amazing!" Cathy and the others tried to see what the book was.

"Did you know that suicide is the second leading cause of death for teenagers?"

Cathy and the others just waited, not sure what to say.

"Doesn't that amaze you?" Sarah said. "Isn't it terrible?"

Sarah didn't seem upset about it, in fact she was the opposite. The information seemed to thrill her. She started to ramble on about more statistics from her book, how suicide was socially acceptable with teens now, how it was an epidemic.

"Why do you care?" Eilean said at last, trying to stop the barrage.

"Of course I care! This is about kids like us." Sarah said. They had found a table by then and were ready to eat. Sarah hadn't even brought a lunch.

"Sorry," Jamie said. "Not kids like us. More like kids with serious mental defects!"

"Wrong!" Sarah said it so loud that other kids turned to look. "It is people like us, normal people. Come on, Jamie! Don't tell me you've never thought about it."

"Me? Never!" He looked embarrassed and gave her a look.

"Yeah, right!" she replied. "What about after you'd been pushed around for like the fiftieth day in a row by those bullies? Remember? They kept pulling down your pants in gym, day after day. You didn't even want to get out of bed anymore, you were so scared!"

Jamie flushed, embarrassed and angry. He leaned closer to her. "I told you that in secret. You said you'd never say anything!" They all knew that he had a crush on Sarah, that he told her things he would never tell anyone else. For that matter, Cathy did the same. There was something about Sarah that made you want to tell her things. Even though it sometimes backfired on you.

"Oh please, Jamie," Sarah said. "It's just the four of us here."

That didn't seem to calm Jamie. Sarah turned away and opened the book to a page she had high-lighted. She started to read out loud.

"Would you put that stupid book away?" Eilean said.

"Why? This is totally cool stuff. Just listen. Boys like really violent ways, like guns and …"

"We're trying to eat here," Cathy laughed.

"Come on you guys!" Sarah replied. "This affects

all of us. I mean, even Eilean's mother …" Sarah stopped, as if realising what she had said.

"Shut up!" Eilean screamed, standing up. This time practically the whole cafeteria looked over. Eilean glared at Sarah. "Don't ever talk about my mother!" All of them knew that Eilean's mother had died a long time ago and it was never mentioned, but this was the first hint they'd had as to why.

With that, Eilean ran to the exit. Cathy wanted to follow her, Jamie glanced over and she knew he wanted to as well. They were torn between their two friends. Instead, they sat there and let Sarah ramble on. Near the end of lunch that day Sarah had said something very odd, after realizing no one really shared her new enthusiasm.

"I guess you can't relate to this stuff unless you've experienced death." Sarah had closed her book and walked away, leaving Cathy and Jamie alone at the table.

"That was a bit dramatic," Jamie said, grinning. "Even for Sarah."

Cathy shook her head. "Yeah. Like, who'd she ever know that died?"

She still didn't know what Sarah had meant that day.

Cathy looked around and saw she had already reached the trail leading to the lower falls. She was out of breath, and her calf muscles were beginning to burn.

She sat on a rock outcropping, just above the trail and pulled her sketchbook from her backpack.

It would be a little while before the tourists arrived. Surrounding her were the steep walls of the gorge, the clear river water rushing below, pine trees clinging to mere inches of dirt, perched on the edge of the granite rock face. To her left was a smooth cavern, carved out of rock by the force of the falls, that tourists walked through to get a better look at the waterfall. A series of barricades made sure that they didn't fall in. Here the waterfall was only a few metres high, not enough to be dangerous in itself. What was dangerous was the force of the water swirling endlessly down through the rest of the gorge. Even in the middle of the coldest winter, the water was too fast for ice to form. She had sketched the falls in all kinds of weather.

She leafed through the pages of her sketchbook, watching the past year unfold. Here were drawings of her grandmother, a still life of the desk in her bedroom; a comical sketch of Jamie dressed as a cowboy. She smiled at this, remembering he had only agreed to pose for her if she would draw him like that. Sarah had seen it and said he looked more like an accountant than a cowboy, and for a while she called him the "Calculator Kid." Her smile faded thinking about Jamie and Sarah, so she tried not to think about them. She had more important things to do.

Taking a deep breath to help clear her mind, she continued through the sketchbook, examining several watercolours she had made at this very spot not long before. She evaluated her technique, trying to be objective. She thought they were still a little crude, but she knew they were getting better. A month or so ago she had discussed her work with Mrs Summers. Cathy had finally confessed to Summers that her real ambition was to be an artist, an illustrator for kids' books, and the kind of artist whose prints end up in galleries and are sold in calendars every Christmas. There was no other teacher whose opinion Cathy valued more.

"Well," Mrs Summers had said at last, "that's quite a dream. You should know it won't be easy. Becoming a successful artist takes determination and a lot of luck. Maybe you should have a backup plan as well, like medicine or law. Something practical."

Cathy nodded and closed her sketchbook, knowing what Mrs Summers really meant. She was too nice to tell her that she wasn't good enough to make it as an artist. She didn't think Cathy was good enough to even teach art. Now was the first time Cathy had opened the sketchbook since that conversation. She had missed most of her art classes since then as well, always making up some excuse.

She thought again about Sarah and Jamie and wondered what had happened. She closed the book, put it back into the backpack and stood, ready for her hike to the upper falls. Up there she knew that the descent was much steeper, the water rushing over a permanent wall of granite and blue ice. The lower falls would do the trick, but it could take a while. The upper falls were more definite, more ... final.

Besides, who needed all these grave-nudgers around to watch?

Chapter 7
Ron

Sarah? Did she really say it was Sarah?

He just sat there, stunned. Shouts in the hall snapped him out of the shock. He saw his lighter lying on the ground, leaving a smoky patch on the tiles. In his surprise, Ron had simply dropped it. The lighter had been his grandfather's and was army issue, built to withstand a hurricane. His grandfather had died in a freak hunting accident when Ron was three or four.

Quickly, he picked it up and stuffed it back in his jacket pocket. He rushed to the door and nearly crashed into Robertson, who was shouting at Eilean. Robertson grabbed Ron by the arm. Ron stopped and glared at him, and Robertson let go. He ran after Eilean and heard Robertson shouting threats behind him.

Who cares? he thought savagely. I'm through with this place. They can do whatever they want to me.

He rushed down the empty hall.

What was Eilean Mull doing in detention? Isn't she one of those perfect students? The ones who never did anything to stick out? And what was she doing there today? The school was closed. And didn't they care that she was Sarah's best friend?

Sarah, he thought, feeling his gut twist again.

Not her. Not Sarah. She was stronger than that.

Ron remembered the blonde girl waiting outside the auditorium. He had only caught a glimpse of her, but he was sure it had been Sarah.

How could they say it was her if he had seen her in the hall less than forty minutes ago? He had to tell Eilean what he'd seen. Tell her that someone made a mistake. Sarah was okay. She had to be.

Ron picked up is pace, wanting to catch up with Eilean.

She was already outside when he finally spotted her. She ran through the staff parking area, heading to the playing field behind it. Eilean was well ahead but he was taller and faster and caught up to her easily. They were on the red clay track when he grabbed her arm.

"Eilean!" he said, panting. "Wait up. I have to tell you …"

"Get away from me!" she sobbed, pulling her arm free. "Just leave me alone!"

She started walking quickly away. He followed her, keeping a few feet back.

"I just wanted to tell you something!"

She started to walk even faster. He kept up easily.

"I saw her this morning. In the hall."

She still ignored him. "Are you deaf or what? I said I saw Sarah this morning!"

She stopped and looked at him. "What? When did you see her?"

"Just before assembly. I saw her in the hall, over by the lockers."

She had looked a little brighter, a little hopeful. Now it was gone.

"You couldn't have," she said. "She'd already done it by then!"

He thought for a moment.

Had he seen wrong? It was just a quick look.

He had to face it. He'd been seeing Sarah everywhere since September. And he always just imagined it.

Ron rubbed his eyes.

Not this time. This time he knew he'd seen her.

"I'm positive it was her," he said. For a moment, Eilean just stared at him, and he saw how pale she was, her eyes red and swollen. She walked toward him, raising her arms. She pushed him. Hard. He was surprised more than hurt and staggered backwards, nearly losing his footing on the clay.

"What kind of person are you?" she yelled. She raised her arms to hit him again and he grabbed her. She swore and shouted at him as she tried to get free.

"You think it's funny?"

"Of course not," he said.

"Don't you get it? If I am right, if I did see her this morning, then it wasn't her they found, right?"

"It's her, you idiot! They didn't make a mistake!"

He let go of her and she walked away. He followed.

"I'm saying that maybe they got it wrong." He spoke quickly as they walked. They had left the school property now and were heading east. A few students were still milling around the school property.

"Maybe whoever found her didn't really know her."

Eilean stopped. "Klein found her. Sarah hanged herself in Klein's office!" Eilean started to walk again and this time he didn't follow. There was a bus stop only a few feet away. He walked over to it and sat heavily on the bench. He felt cold and numb, his thoughts racing. A long time seemed to go by before he heard a voice speaking to him. He looked up and saw Eilean standing over him.

"What?"

"I asked you what's the matter?" Eilean replied.

He shook his head. "Nothing."

"You look terrible," Eilean said. "Is it because of Sarah?"

Ron looked at the ground.

"Why do you care?" she asked.

A voice inside him said: Tell her — you need to tell someone.

He rubbed his face and looked away. Years of keeping thoughts and feelings deep inside stopped him. He couldn't open up now. Not to Eilean. He didn't really know her.

"It doesn't matter," he said, shaking his head. She stared at him for a moment. "Jesus. I guess Klein really did a number on her."

"What does that mean? What do you know about her and Klein?"

"You know. All that drug crap, kicking her out of school. I mean, doing it in Klein's office, that's got to be sending a message. Right?"

Eilean's expression said she was trying to decide what he had really meant to say. Finally she looked up at the clear sky and he saw fresh tears on her cheeks.

"I'd already thought about that," she said softly.

He stood up thinking: What do I do? What do I say to her?

He had no reference point, no way of knowing how to act in a situation like this. He thought of his father, knowing how he would respond to anyone showing the least sign of weakness. Even a child would be treated with contempt and sarcasm. Ron just stood next to Eilean, feeling helpless.

"What are you going to do?" he asked her finally, to break the silence. She shrugged.

"Do you want to go home? I could give you a ride. My car's right over by the ..."

"Why do you want to help me?"

He couldn't tell her it was because she was Sarah's friend, and he'd do anything for Sarah.

"I don't know," he said. "Why not?"

"You don't even know me."

"I've seen you around."

She seemed to mull this over for a moment or two.

"Alright. I want to go to the hospital. I have to find out how Sarah is."

Ron's heart leapt into his throat.

"What now?" she asked. "You said you wanted to help me."

He wanted to help her, but not that. Not the hospital. Ron had no idea why he felt this way, but the thought of going there, seeing Sarah injured or worse ... he couldn't bear it.

What if he went there and Sarah was okay? What then? Would she still reject him like she had all year?

"But her parents will be there," he said. "And the hospital probably won't let us anywhere near her."

"Then we'll make them."

Ron still hesitated, still not sure why it scared him to see Sarah.

"Fine!" she said turning away. "I'll get there myself." She started to walk away and Ron knew he had to act.

"Okay! I'll take you." She didn't bother to look as Ron fell in step beside her. "Look, I meant what I said. I want to help. I just don't think they'll tell us anything."

"We can at least try, right?"

He nodded. "My car's back here."

Chapter 8
Eilean

Eilean had been a bit surprised when they reached his car. She didn't know a lot about cars, but she was sure this one was new and expensive. It was all the more surprising since Ron always dressed like such a slob.

"Is this yours?" she asked. He only shrugged and mumbled something about it being a present.

As they drove, in silence, Eilean wondered why he was acting so strangely. It didn't seem like the Ron Freis she'd always seen.

It took less than ten minutes to reach the hospital. Eilean had no idea if this was the right one, but it was the closest. As she rushed inside, she spotted Sarah's parents standing in a corner of the emergency room.

Eilean felt a rush of emotion at seeing them. She had always been close to Sarah's mom and had spent more time at the Spokes's house than at her own growing up. That was one more thing Sarah took away these last few months, she thought, she kept me away from her mother as well. Eilean walked quickly, feeling the sudden need to hold her, and to be held.

"Hurry!" she called to Ron, who lagged behind. He sped up a little until he noticed where she was heading. He grabbed her by the arm.

"Are those her parents?"

"Yeah," Eilean replied, wondering how he'd guessed that. She supposed it was Sarah's resemblance to her mom. Then she wondered how he would know anything about Sarah.

"I don't think I can do this."

"Whatever," she said, fed up with his behaviour. "Thanks for the lift."

"I'll wait for you," he said. "In case you need a ride home."

She stared at him. This was the great Ron Freis, tough guy. He looked just like a lost boy. Why was he being so nice?

"It's okay," she said at last. "I could be here a while."

He nodded, shoving his hands in the pockets of his old leather jacket.

"Sure," he said. "Whatever." He stood there and Eilean turned away, heading over to Sarah's parents. They were still in shock, standing in the middle of the emergency room, staring off. Eilean found herself slowing down slightly, not sure what to say to them. As she approached, she saw Sarah's mother turn and spot her. Debbie Spokes's face had been blank, her cheeks pale and tear-stained. Now, as she turned and saw Eilean approach, her face changed, and Eilean saw the anger. At first she thought she was wrong, that it was just concern, then she thought that Sarah's mother was angry at something else.

"You!" she shouted. "What are you doing here?"

Eilean stopped dead, the rage frightening her. Sarah's dad turned to see who was there. Sarah's mother started to rush at Eilean, hands raised to strike.

What is going on? Eilean thought. Why is she doing this?

Sarah's dad grabbed his wife, holding her back.

"How dare you come here!" Mrs Spokes hissed.

"Mrs Spokes," Eilean began. "Debbie. What ..."

Before she could finish, Sarah's mother was shouting again, moving closer despite her husband's effort to restrain her.

"Don't, Deb!" her husband said. "Not now!"

"Why not now? She's the reason our baby is lying there!" She wrenched one arm free of her husband's grasp and pointed to the room behind her.

Eilean was stunned. "Me? But, how is this my fault?"

She didn't get it. Did Mrs Spokes think she was someone else? But that was insane — they'd known each other all Eilean's life.

"Don't act stupid with us! You knew the whole time what she was planning!"

Eilean started to speak, but couldn't think of anything to say. She was too surprised, too shocked to think clearly.

"The teacher told us, the one who found my baby this morning. She said that all of you were in some kind of sick pact! How could you do it?"

Eilean felt her own anger grow. It had been building all morning, after the news about Sarah, after the way she had been treated by the school. Now Sarah's mother stood there blaming her for all of this! And Klein! It seemed that everything bad these days had something to do with Klein.

"Me?" she shouted back. "Why couldn't *you* see it coming? Are you that blind? You couldn't see that something was wrong with Sarah?"

"Don't tell me how to be a mother! If you were any kind of friend you wouldn't have got Sarah mixed up in something this sickening!"

"You think it was me?" Eilean replied. "You're actually blaming me? You think I can tell Sarah what to do?"

"Shut up! Both of you!" Sarah's father shouted. They ignored him.

"All these months, everything that's happened, and you kept pretending everything was perfect!" Eilean shouted.

It started to get worse; both of them screaming at each other, getting closer and closer, their rage and their sorrow blinding them, making them say terrible things. And then Ron appeared. He stood between Eilean and the Spokeses, glaring at them.

Even Eilean had to step back — this was the Ron Freis she had seen before. This was the Ron who had terrified half the school for years.

"Back off, both of you!"

Sarah's parents looked at him, momentarily silenced by his appearance. Ron turned to Eilean.

"Let's get out of here."

"I want to see Sarah!"

"This isn't the time." He nodded at something over her shoulder. She saw a nurse escorting two uniformed guards. It was clear they were heading in their direction.

"I'm not finished here! She thinks I did this!"

"You didn't. Now let's go!"

He grabbed her by the arm and started to drag her out of the hospital. She resisted for a moment, before giving in. She wanted to get away from there as much as he did. As they rushed to the doors, she heard Sarah's mother shouting again. This time at Ron.

"I know you!" she said. "I've seen you with Sarah!"

"Wrong guy, lady," Ron said. Then they were outside, past the automatic doors and walking quickly toward his car. Eilean looked back once and saw the two guards watching them from the doorway. At his car, Ron opened the passenger door and practically threw her inside. He rushed to his side, slid in, started the car and sped off. He slammed on the brakes when he nearly collided with an ambulance.

"Calm down! Before you get us killed!"

"*Me* calm down? What about back there? What was that all about?"

Eilean looked away, crossing her arms. She wasn't sure what had happened herself. Ron pulled the car into an empty spot and killed the engine. They both just sat there for a while, neither saying a word.

"What now?" he asked at last.

"All I wanted was to see her, make sure she was okay."

"I know. But that's not going to happen right now."

Eilean sat there in silence once more. She had no idea what to do now. She thought of Klein, always meddling, always managing to make a bad situation worse. Then she thought of this morning, remembering something Klein had said in the vice-principal's office.

"Klein told me something this morning. This theory she had."

"Who cares what Klein thinks?" Ron said.

"This time I believe her." She looked at Ron. "Can you drive me someplace? To get a friend?"

"Where is this friend?"

"I don't know."

* * *

"You don't have any idea where she might have gone?" Ron asked her for at least the tenth time.

"I already told you, I don't have a clue!"

72

They were driving slowly through a school zone and she looked out her passenger window at the school grounds. It was lunch and the kids were running around, screaming and playing. Lucky little punks, she thought. Enjoy it while you can. Life only gets worse.

"Look, this is pointless. She could be anywhere. What about a mall?"

"Yeah, right! Cathy hanging in a mall all by herself. That isn't exactly her idea of a good time."

"Well, how am I supposed to know that?"

Again and again, Eilean tried to think of some logical place Cathy might go to be alone, but nothing came to mind. Over the past few months, she had barely seen Cathy. All this talk of death had sickened Eilean. She remembered what Klein had said, her theory about Eilean's mother. She knew deep down that was the reason she had been drifting away from the others, that a line had been crossed.

The tension between Eilean and Ron was growing. He was upset about something, she saw, though he refused to talk about it. Her frustration and fear had also grown after their search had lead down one dead end after another.

Even trying to reach her father had been frustrating. She had called him on her cellphone. He had picked up almost immediately.

"Eilean?"

"Dad, it's me! Listen …!" She had heard him start to speak again when there was a beep and the line went dead. The LED on her phone read: signal lost. After several attempts, she finally gave up, knowing that his plane was in some remote area up north. She hoped that he had heard her before the signal was lost. It was good to hear his voice, even for just a second.

"This is stupid," Ron said again.

Eilean kept her mouth shut and tried to think. She had begun to bite her nails, something she hadn't done since she was a little girl. The knot in her stomach was constant and she kept shifting in her seat, more scared than she could ever remember being.

They had first tried going to Cathy's house. That had been a little too intense. Cathy's mother had come to the door, looking pale and worried.

"Eilean," she had said. "Where's Cathy?"

"We came to see if she was here."

"The school called. They told me about Sarah and the boy."

Cathy's mother could never remember Jamie's name, had never liked the idea of a boy hanging out so much with girls. Cathy in particular.

"What did they say to you about Cathy?"

"They asked to talk to Cathy, but I told them she had already gone to school." Cathy's mother looked near tears. "That's what I thought she had done."

"Mrs. Chen, are you sure she's not at home? Maybe in the tub or still in her room or something?"

"Of course she's not home! I looked everywhere. The car's gone, too!"

Eilean thought she had never seen someone in so much despair before. "The police are looking for her now. I can't believe this is happening."

Eilean put a hand on her shoulder. "We'll keep looking for her."

"You tell her to come home right away!"

With that, she closed the door. Eilean and Ron turned and headed back to his car.

"I didn't expect that," he said.

"What?"

"Cathy's mom. I thought she'd have an accent or something."

Eilean gave him another warning glance. "Great. Not only are you a bully, you're a racist as well."

"I'm not a racist!" he said, climbing behind the wheel. "I just thought she'd have an accent."

That had been nearly two hours ago and they were no closer to figuring out where Cathy might be, or even if she was really in trouble. After all, the suicide pact had been Klein's suggestion. For all they knew she was at the library, or sneaking off somewhere with a boy.

The latter idea seemed a little far-fetched to Eilean. As far as she knew, Cathy was still terrified of all boys. All boys with the exception of Jamie Seilig, that is. Thinking of Jamie brought a rush of memories back, most of them from the days when they were best friends, before Sarah started to go strange. The thought of all of them together triggered a flash of memory. What was it? What had she seen recently?

"Look, we've been driving around forever and you haven't even told me why you're all so worried about this Cathy chick."

"Just give me a minute," she said, a little louder than she meant to. She almost had the memory and needed Ron to keep quiet.

That's it! The picture! The one of all four of them up at Chinaman's Gorge! How many times had Cathy raved about the place, telling them over and over how it was her most favourite place to go? That had to be it.

"We have to drive to Banff!"

"Banff?" Ron said. "Are you nuts?"

"That's were she is! I know it!"

"I don't have enough gas to go to Banff," Ron said. "And I'm broke."

"I'll give you the gas money. Let's just go!"

"Not until you tell me what's going on."

"We're running out of time. And you said you wanted to help me, right?"

"Yeah. But you didn't tell me I'd have to be a tour guide!" He said, adding a few choice swear words.

"Look," she said, knowing she had to tell him everything. "You already know about Sarah. What she did. Another friend of mine killed himself."

"What," he shouted, looking over at her. "Who?"

She hesitated a moment, keeping her emotions in check.

"Jamie Seilig."

Ron shook his head. "When was this?"

"Last night. Powers told me this morning. He told me that kids sometimes form suicide pacts. They thought I might be in on it. That's why they had me stuck in detention."

Ron's face had gone pale. "This is totally insane!"

"I know. But it's the truth."

"And you think this Cathy is in on it?"

"Sarah had this weird control over both of them. And Cathy is missing. She's never gone missing in her life!"

Ron looked ahead while they waited at a red light. He seemed to be thinking it all over. Eilean bit her tongue, her heart racing wildly as she waited for his decision.

"Are you in on it?" he asked.

She looked at him. "No."

The light turned green and he stepped on the peddle. "There's a gas station at the next corner. We can fill up there."

Eilean nodded.

"Thanks." As they pulled up to the pumps, she turned her head away from him.

Inwardly she begged, Hold on, Cath! Please. We'll be there soon.

Eilean hoped that soon was soon enough.

Chapter 9
Cathy

Jamie.

Where did that come from? Why did his face suddenly pop into her head?

After a few moments, still climbing the steep trail, Cathy managed to blank him out again. She was finally on the last part of the trail leading to the upper falls, and the mist was thick here. The trail was covered with powdery red clay that left tiny clouds of dust with each footfall. Whiskey-jacks shrieked in the densely packed pines that bordered the trail. Sometimes the trees thinned enough to catch a glimpse of the misty sky or the jagged edge of the trail falling sharply to the canyon below. She was out of breath, partly because of her backpack, partly because of the thin air this high in the mountains.

Oh, admit it, she told herself, you're also pretty out of shape!

She almost smiled at that. Oh well, another New Year's resolution shot. The good thing about her decision was that she didn't have to worry about failing any more resolutions.

Cathy needed to rest. She spotted a narrow deer track and followed it until she was out of sight of the main trail. There she sat on the stump of a fallen tree and watched the rushing water far below, heard it crash as it swept through the canyon walls. For some reason, the mental fog she had been in all morning was beginning to clear. Maybe it was the exertion of the hike, or maybe it was something else.

Years ago, in one of her first classes with Mrs Summers, they had tried a focus exercise. Each of the students had cut a rectangle out of some white cardboard and been told to draw only what they saw inside that small area. Cathy had loved it, finding it helped her picture small details.

That was how it had been this morning. The world outside her little rectangle didn't matter.

As she sat on the stump, the world seemed to open up around her, slowly. First she felt her ragged breathing, the pain in her calves and the beginning of a blister on her right heel. Then the sounds of the forest began to seep through the edge of her small window. She wondered what had happened this morning, how everything had turned out for Sarah and Jamie. She hoped that they were at peace now.

As Sarah had become more of a leader than a friend, Cathy and Jamie had become closer, telling each other everything.

Well, nearly everything. A girl had to have her secrets.

When he had told her that Sarah frightened him sometimes, Cathy was relieved to hear she wasn't the only one who felt that way. A few weeks ago he told her about the night Sarah had shown up in his room, what had happened. Cathy tried to make him feel better, and for a moment, she thought she could hate Sarah for treating him that way.

"It's not that I didn't want to," he said. "It's just that she surprised me."

Cathy nodded, letting him explain, let it out.

"I'm not scared of girls. And I do like girls, you know that."

This is it, she thought. I finally got my opening.

"There's one way to find out for sure," she said.

"How?"

"Well, I don't scare you, do I?"

Jamie grinned. She loved his grin.

"Of course not."

"Then kiss me," she said, amazed she found the courage to say it out loud. Jamie looked at her, surprised. Then he started to laugh.

"Get real!" he said. "You're my best friend! That'd be like kissing my sister or something." She laughed with him.

Jamie, I couldn't let you know you broke my heart.

Cathy stood and walked back to the main trail. It was still empty. She had been right about the bus group not coming this far. They rarely did. Either they were too old to make the climb or the driver rushed them along, anxious to get to the next attraction.

It took another fifteen minutes or so of climbing before she reached the entrance to the upper falls. At the end of the trail was a set of high wooden stairs, leading up to the metal observation deck. There were only a few people here, including a tall, athletic-looking blonde couple. They stood on the observation deck, sipping bottled water and admiring the falls on the opposite side of the gorge, less than twenty metres away. There was also a family with two young kids in tow, including a baby strapped to the mother's back. Everyone was damp from the spray.

As she walked along the path, the tall blonde woman looked back and smiled at her. It was something Cathy had seen before. The long, tiring hike would create a group spirit amongst those who made it this far. Cathy just wiped her hair from her eyes and pretended not to see her.

Here at the end of the trail, the falls rushed over the cliff face on the opposite side of the gorge. There was a tall metal barricade that stopped the tourists from getting too close to the edge. When she had first come here, it was only about a half-metre high. Now a loose metal mesh extended up more than ten metres, secured by metal pegs bored into the canyon wall. Rock climbers had started to come here to try the slippery face, even though there were much better places to climb. One climber had been killed, swept into the gorge below, and so the park had erected the mesh barricade. The new structure blocked only the area the climbers had preferred. It didn't block the entire area. Cathy knew it made her plan a little tougher, but not impossible.

You'll have to wait, she told herself, if you don't want an audience.

She sat on a rock far from the barricade and pulled the sketchbook from her backpack. She also pulled out her tin of pencil crayons, purely by reflex. She looked at the pencils, wondering why she'd brought them. She wasn't here to sketch.

Cathy took in the sights surrounding her, the roaring water, the thick blue ice shelf just to the right of it, the sheer rock cropping above it all. To her left, far above the falls, were steep alpine meadows, dotted with colourful wild flowers and coarse grass. The meadow grass was a lush green, permanently damp from the spray.

Once, she had seen a grizzly up there, chewing on something and staring down at the humans lined up to see the waterfall. She had been the only one to spot the bear, and at first she turned to tell the others. But she stopped, wanting to keep the bear for herself. She had stared at it until it slowly wandered out of sight, its silver coat shimmering in the late afternoon sun.

"That is a very nice drawing," someone said behind her. Cathy looked up, startled, not having been aware anyone was there. She saw that it was the tall blonde woman she had seen earlier. She had a thick accent Cathy couldn't quite place. German, she thought, or maybe Swedish. She certainly looked like one of those typical blonde

82

giants you see on television travel shows.

"Thanks," she said quietly. She never knew how to react to compliments. She hoped the woman would go away.

But the woman stayed where she was.

"You have more?" she asked. It took a few seconds for Cathy to understand what she had asked.

"What? Oh, yes. A few."

"May I look?"

Cathy watched as the woman crouched near her, holding out a hand toward the sketchbook, smiling at her. Cathy didn't know what to do at first. She didn't want to talk to anyone; she wanted to be alone.

The woman seemed to think that Cathy's hesitation was shyness. She smiled again and reached into her own backpack, pulling out a small sketch pad carefully wrapped in a waterproof pouch. She pulled it free and offered it to Cathy.

"We can trade. Yes?"

Cathy blinked, startled at being pulled further into the world. Without a word, she took the woman's small pad and handed over her own. Taking it eagerly, the woman sat down on a rock near Cathy and opened the book. Cathy watched for a moment and then opened the sketchbook in her hand. It was wonderful. Each page was filled with beautiful sketches, some in colour, most done in pencil.

"Wow!" Cathy blurted out, "these are gorgeous!"

The sketches began with scenes of Europe, flowing into various locations in the Rockies. She knew instantly more than a dozen spots, ones she had drawn herself again and again. It seemed that the woman and Cathy had the same taste.

"These are very good," the woman said, pausing on a sketch of the falls beside them.

"Thanks," she replied, adding, "I love yours," and she meant it.

"Are you a student at the university?"

"No," Cathy said. "Too young." She hesitated. "Besides …" she stopped herself.

"Besides?" The blonde woman asked. "What besides?"

"It's just that I wouldn't make it into art school."

"But why not?"

"Because I'm not good enough."

The blonde woman studied her for a moment. She indicated the sketchbook.

"Nonsense. These are wonderful. Look at how you did the water here, and the sky. You are very skilled."

Cathy smiled. She couldn't help herself. She thought, she's this amazing artist, and she thinks I'm good, too?

"Are you a professional?"

The blonde woman shook her head. "This is just my diary. My husband over there likes his expensive camera, but I always find the pictures disappoint. They are missing the feeling you had when you stood there." She held up the sketchbook and smiled. "But not with these, correct? These capture the moment."

Cathy nodded. She couldn't agree more. She much preferred a drawing to a photograph. They exchanged books again and the woman once more covered hers in the waterproof pouch. After returning it to her backpack, the blonde woman looked at Cathy again, frowning slightly.

"Someone said you were not good?"

Cathy shrugged. "Well, my art teacher …"

"Art teacher!" the woman said, waving a hand dismissively. "What does a teacher know? If they are so good, they would be doing, not teaching! Yes?"

Cathy grinned. I think I really like her, she thought.

They smiled at each other for a few moments and then the woman stood up.

"It was good to meet you. And to see your art."

She leaned down slightly and held out her right hand. Cathy took it and they shook. With a final nod, the blonde woman turned away, heading back to the barricade and the man waiting there. Cathy looked at her sketchbook, and after a few seconds, turned back to the trail. The couple had already disappeared.

Cathy stood and stretched, her back and legs a little stiff from sitting on the cold rocks for so long. She lifted her backpack to her shoulder as she walked to the edge of the falls. A quick look around told her she was alone.

She left the sketchbook lying on the rocks behind her.

Cathy stuck her left boot into the mesh of the barricade and began to climb, the mesh wobbling crazily as she tried to cling to it. It took a few minutes to clear it and reach the rock above. She began scrambling to find a grip on the smooth rock face. Clutching pine roots and clumps of coarse grass, she pulled herself up the side of the canyon wall, her hair sticking to her face and getting into her eyes. She was out of breath as she reached a ledge and crouched there, feeling her legs and arms tremble from the exertion of the climb. After several minutes, she felt a bit better and her breathing returned to normal. She tossed her backpack over the edge and watched it tumble against the sheer granite walls before the rush of water took it. At first, the force of the water tugged it deep into the river, and it disappeared from sight. She kept watching and soon saw it burst through the water, tumbling and tossing, following the path of the river south toward the bottom of the gorge.

She looked at her hands, the nails filthy and broken, the fingers and palms covered in scratches.

Focus, Cathy. Don't let a little pain stop you now. It's almost over.

As she inspected her wounds, she saw that she had also torn the sleeve of her fleece jacket from cuff to elbow. Cathy balanced herself on the narrow rock shelf and slipped the jacket off. She hung it over the edge and let it dangle for a moment before letting go. It fluttered down into the mist and water much more slowly than her backpack had. The water took it and sucked it down beneath the surface. It never emerged again. Cathy looked back down at the mesh railing a few feet below her, and beyond that, to the rush of water blasting through the gorge.

She stood up, wiped the wet hair from her eyes and lifted her right foot, letting it dangle in the mist and empty space between her and the unimaginable force of rushing water.

Chapter 10
Ron

Ron sped up to 140 kph to pass a slow-moving Winnebago. He let the speed drop down to 125 as he eased back into the westbound lane. It was still quite a bit over the speed limit, but he knew he had to get to Banff as quickly as possible. He smiled a little, knowing that something like a speeding ticket wouldn't normally worry him. But not today. If he was stopped now it could be fatal.

Traffic had been heavy for a weekday, with what looked like retirees heading for British Columbia in gigantic motor homes or pulling campers. Eilean had been silent the whole trip, sitting with her legs pulled up to her chin, looking out the passenger window. He could tell from the quick glances he stole that she was crying off and on.

He couldn't imagine it. Finding out that one of your best friends was dead. Another one just hanging in there.

He wanted to tell her that he was thinking of

Sarah too. He wanted to tell her of the guilt he felt, how miserable he was about not trying to help Sarah last fall, when things got so bad for her. He wasn't really surprised to see that Eilean had no clue, that Sarah had never mentioned what happened last summer.

* * *

It had been a long day and he was exhausted, driving home in the pouring rain. Ron had just finished at his part-time job at the local Dairy Queen, after a full day at his other job. Right after school was over, he had managed to get a summer job at a warehouse not far from home, loading and unloading semis all day. It was hard work but the pay wasn't bad. The worst part of the warehouse job was sitting at the lunch table with all the other workers, most of them high school dropouts who would work there until they retired or broke their backs. The conversations were mind-deadening. Of course, he really needed the money, since his old man had cut off his allowance on his sixteenth birthday.

"Your mother and I have been supporting your juvenile habits long enough. You're sixteen, old enough to get some part-time work and pay for your own Slurpees and CDs and God knows what else you buy."

His mother had made her usual feeble protest, more of a show these days than anything else. Her husband ran the house, and made sure they all knew it. Ron knew better than to protest once the old man made a proclamation like that. The next day, Ron had bought his own newspaper and had gone carefully through the ads, looking for work. There had been one pleasant benefit to his finding work after school — he saw less of his old man. All through the rest of the school year he had worked after school at various jobs, flipping burgers or delivering pizzas, anything he could find.

It had been a Friday night and he knew that his lazy-ass friends would be having a party at Fritz's house since his parents had gone to the mountains for the weekend. Fritz had convinced them that since he was nearly seventeen, he was old enough to take care of himself. Somehow his parents had agreed, and the house was now the party place until late Sunday.

He stopped at a red light, where he saw a girl standing at the bus stop. She had no umbrella and didn't seem to notice the rain soaking her. Something about her was familiar and he leaned across the passenger seat to roll down the window for a better look.

I know her, he thought. She'd been kind of hot back in junior high. Popular as well. Then she'd gone nuts or something, started hanging out with losers.

"Hey," he shouted, taking a chance. "You want a lift?"

The girl ignored him. What the hell was her name? Susan? Sharon. He got it.

"Hey, Sarah! It's okay. It's me, Ron. From school."

She crouched down a little to see him better. Under the harsh light of the street light, he could see that her cheeks were flushed even in this downpour.

"Get lost!" she said at last.

"Come on, it's pouring! Get in! I'm not dangerous."

She looked at him again. "I am."

Whoo-ho! he thought, a little fighter, this one. Who'da thunk it.

"I'm going to a party. It's gonna be wild!"

"I don't fit in with your crowd."

"That's in school. We're not in school right now."

She looked up at the pouring rain. "So I noticed."

"Come on," he said. "What else were you gonna do tonight? Go home and watch reruns?"

She looked down the street as if to see if a bus was anywhere in sight, then looked back at Ron and smiled. He opened the door and she slipped inside along with the pouring rain. She slammed the door shut and looked at him, wiping her wet blonde hair from her eyes.

"Just to let you know, you try anything and I swear I'll mess you up."

He saw a look in her eye, a weird glow to her skin. For a second he thought about stopping the car, telling her to get out again. Just for a second.

But the moment passed and they were off, heading to Fritz's and the wild party he had promised her.

As they drove along, she stared at him openly, not even trying to hide it. The frankness of her gaze freaked him out a bit, and he tried to keep his mind on driving.

"What?" he said at last.

"Nothing," she said. "I was just admiring your outfit."

He looked down and grinned. He was still wearing his work uniform. He didn't bother to tell her that he had his trunks on underneath, ready to hit the pool as soon as possible.

The party that night was wild, but she was wilder. None of the guys could believe this was the same girl they had seen in school, the smart one, the kind that joined the student council, involved in everything. As soon as they arrived, she grabbed a beer from the ice-filled bucket on Fritz's patio, downed half in one gulp and then jumped into the pool. The rain had stopped by then and the party was slowly moving outside.

"What the hell are you doing?" Fritz shouted at her, grinning at the fully clothed girl paddling in the deep end, still holding the beer bottle.

"Why not?" she shouted. "I was wet anyway!"

Fritz looked over at Ron. "Where did you meet this chick?"

"At school," Ron replied, grabbing his own beer.

Fritz swore. "Yeah, right! I would have noticed her!"

"You're too busy pulling down guys' pants in gym to notice any chicks!"

Fritz swore again, giving Ron a punch in the arm. "I gotta meet her."

"Too late. I saw her first."

"We'll see about that," Fritz said grinning.

What the hell did that mean? Ron wondered. Fritz had never let a chick come between them.

He looked over at the wet girl splashing around in the pool, whooping.

"Hey!" she yelled over at Ron, holding up her empty beer bottle. "Get me another one!"

He grinned at her, grabbed a bottle from the ice and began to run, jumping into the pool beside her, not bothering to take off his uniform. She laughed and grabbed him by the arm, snatching the beer from his hand.

She slid an arm around him and pulled him closer.

"Thanks for the drink," she said, taking a gulp. "I think I want some Freis with that."

She pulled him closer and kissed him. The others started to whoop and they broke apart, laughing.

"I guess you have your uses after all," she said, her face only inches from his.

"I got lots of uses," he replied. They stared at each other and then she swam away, finishing the beer. He started to swim toward her, just as everyone else at the party jumped in, nearly all of them fully clothed. For a few moments, he lost her in the splashing water, the screams and laughter, the general mess of a few dozen bodies in a pool at the same time. He felt a hand slip across his neck and turned to see Sarah staring at him. The two beers she had downed didn't seem to have deadened the strange gleam in her eyes. She swam across him and wrapped her arms around his neck, her legs around his waist.

"Let's par-tay!" she said, softly.

That had been early July, and for the rest of the summer, he and Sarah had kept up the strangest relationship he'd ever been in. They saw each other often; he even quit his night job to spend more time with her. Most of that summer she had been up, with that crazy look in her eyes. At these times she was ready to try anything, go anywhere, her excitement so extreme that sometimes he even tried to hold her back. Then there were days when she wouldn't return his calls and stayed in her room without speaking to anyone. On those days, if he did manage to speak to her, she would either be angry at him or so lazy it was like she was half-awake.

And then there were the drugs. She had insisted that it was her summer to break free, to stop being the good girl, always worrying about what others thought of her. Between himself and his friends, he made some connections, people that even he was scared to be in the same room with. Sarah didn't care, she wanted to finally experience all the things she had been too scared to do before.

Sarah brought him along to the next level. She

had this way of clearing things up, of making sense of the craziest ideas.

The summer continued on this way, with Sarah happy and wild, or miserable, refusing to come out of her house. He lost his job at the warehouse, being fired for always coming in either late or too hung-over to work. There had been arguments at home, the old man trying to order him to stay in, to quit whatever he was up to every night. When they tried to ground him, he ignored them. Only Sarah had power over him.

Then there was the hot August night when he called her after she'd disappeared into her house once again. Her mother answered the phone, and he could tell how upset she was.

"You're the boy she's been seeing all summer," she said, not passing the phone on to Sarah. He had said he was.

"She won't even tell us your name, never mind bring you to the house." She said it like it was his fault, his choice. He didn't like her tone, but he kept his mouth shut.

"I don't know what's wrong with her these days. It's like she's a different person. You're a bad influence on her. I'm warning you to stay away or I'll find out who you are and go see your parents."

The mother was just as nuts as the daughter, he thought.

She hung up on him and he never tried to call the house again.

Ron had stayed up late, arguing with Sarah's

mother in his head: How would you like it, old woman, if I told you the truth? How would you like it if you knew your precious daughter was the wild one, taking me along for the ride?

It didn't matter in the end. Sarah hadn't spoken to him again. School started a few days later and she acted like she didn't know him. She ignored him in the halls, and when he tried to pull her aside to talk, to find out what he'd done wrong, she refused to answer.

"It's finished," she said. "Stop being a little boy. Get over it!"

With that she walked away and they never spoke again. He was pissed at first, and then he just missed her. He had wanted to call her up, dozens of times, to apologize for whatever he had done to make her hate him. Mostly, he just wanted to talk to her.

He might never get the chance again.

"Watch it!" Eilean yelled.

Ron focused and saw he had begun to drift into the opposing lane. He straightened out, concentrating on his driving once again. They had passed the exits to Kananaskis, and he knew they were less than forty minutes away from the park gates of Banff.

"Try to concentrate, okay?" Eilean said. "I don't want to die trying to stop someone else from dying."

Chapter 11
Eilean

Stop it! she told herself. Stop thinking about them! It won't do any good now. But she couldn't stop the questions: Why did they do it? Didn't they know how stupid, how useless it is to die this young?

Over and over again, she wondered what she could have done differently. She shook her head. Her first attempt to help Sarah hadn't exactly been a huge success, had it?

Sarah had added drugs to her bizarre behaviour and Eilean had gone to Klein, trusting that the school counsellor would help Sarah. She was wrong. Klein had just called the cops and gotten Sarah suspended

Sarah gave up the drugs, got back into school, but then became obsessed with death, with suicide statistics and methods. That's when Eilean started to distance herself. When Sarah started going on about suicide, it felt like a personal attack.

She remembered thinking: She wants to hurt me. She wants to get back at me for turning her in.

Eilean distanced herself from Sarah and the other two. She told them she didn't need to listen to their horrible little ideas. She told them it was sick, and boring. So Sarah dropped the subject, at least in her presence, but she knew that it was different with Jamie and Cathy. They soaked it up, including the message that their lives were pointless, that things were never going to get better. Eilean saw the photocopies, the notes they passed to one another. It was just that their morbid little fantasies were so pathetic. She had no idea that any of them really would take all the posturing seriously. More than once she had considered telling her dad. She had stopped herself, realizing there was little he could do to help.

More than that, Eilean couldn't bear to bring up the subject, knowing that he still mourned all these years later. She knew how much her father loved her. She knew that he had passed over job offers and promotions in order to stay close, to be there for her as she grew up. Now she was old enough to take care of herself and he'd started thinking about his career again. His work in the oil fields meant a lot of travel, usually only within the province. It still meant that he was away for days at a time, just as he had been when she was a little girl.

She became angry again thinking of Klein and Powers phoning her father, warning him his daughter was about to kill herself. She hated the fact he was on his way back right now, a prisoner of time and distance, praying to arrive in time. Just as she prayed she would arrive in time for Cathy. She knew that for him it was a thousand times worse. It was worse because he had been through it all before.

* * *

Mommy had been sad again. It seemed that her mother was sad most of the time. It was worse when Daddy was away, like he had been that weekend. It had been a very long day, the Sunday before her father was to come home, and Eilean wondered why Mommy wasn't as excited as she was about seeing him again. After a mostly silent supper, interrupted by bouts of silent tears, her mother sent her to bed early, without giving her a bath or insisting she brush her teeth. Eilean lay in bed listening as her mother wandered around the house, cleaning up in the kitchen before running herself a bath. She lay awake for a long time, a knot growing in her stomach, though she had no idea what was upsetting her. As she lay in her bed, she saw out her window that it had started to snow, the beginning of a nasty winter storm. At last she drifted off to sleep.

When she woke the next day, the house was silent. She looked out her bedroom window and saw all the snow, grinning at the fat, wet flakes continuing to fall. She couldn't wait to get outside and play in it. Dressing quickly, she walked into the hall, seeing her mother's bedroom door was shut. She knew that this meant her mother was still asleep and didn't want to be bothered. As quietly as possible, she crept downstairs and into the kitchen. She found a bowl and a box of cereal set out for her, a glass of juice covered with Saran wrap in the fridge, ready for her to drink. Also on the table was her little Fisher-Price recorder. She knew that Mommy and Daddy sometimes left her messages on it. Eilean pressed the big red button and heard her mother's voice. Even on the tape she sounded sad.

"Morning, sweetheart," her mother's voice said. "Breakfast is all ready. You can even make toast if you want to. Please let Mommy sleep. Daddy will be home soon. I love you."

Eilean grinned. She loved it when her parents let her do grown-up things like make her own toast. She grabbed two pieces of bread from the container on the counter and placed them in the toaster. When the toast popped, she rushed to pull it out.

"Ow!" she yelped, not expecting the toast to be so hot. She shouted up to her mother, but there was no response. She picked the toast off the floor, cleaned it off and buttered it. As she ate breakfast alone, the phone rang and she picked it up quickly so the noise wouldn't wake her mother.

"Hello?" she said into the receiver.

"Hello?" she heard her father say. "Eilean? Is that you?"

"Hi, Daddy! Are you coming home now?"

"Not until late, honey," he said.

"But you promised! You said today."

"I know. But the weather is really bad up here. We're all snowed in."

"It's snowing here too, daddy."

"I know. Is Mommy there?"

"She's still asleep. You want me to get her?"

"No that's okay. Just tell her that I'm stuck probably until tonight. Tell her I'll call in a few hours. Can you remember that?"

"Sure."

They said goodbye and Eilean hung up the phone. She looked at the clock, and although she didn't exactly know how to tell time yet, she knew it was later than usual for her mother to be sleeping. She looked outside at the snow falling and really wanted to go out and play. Finally, after waiting as long as she could for her mother to get up, she decided that if she was grown up enough to make toast, she was grown up enough to play outside. She pulled on her snow suit and boots and walked out the back door, ready for winter.

When she came back inside, cold and exhausted, the house was still silent. The TV wasn't on with Mommy's shows, and there wasn't the smell of coffee brewing. As she had come in, she had heard her father's voice and ran into the living room with her boots on, excited. When she got there, she realized he was only leaving a message on the answering machine. She rushed to the phone but was too late; her father had already hung up. Eilean shook off her winter clothes and headed back upstairs to her mother's room. As quietly as she could, she opened the door. The curtains were still closed and it was hard to see as she walked in. As she approached the bed, she saw her mother lying on top of the covers, still sound asleep. Eilean walked up to her and saw that her mother was wearing her prettiest dress and that she had put on make-up.

"Mommy?" she said. There was no response. A little frightened, she reached out to touch her mother's arm, to wake her up. Her mother's skin was cold as ice. A few more attempts to wake her also failed, so after grabbing a quilt from the closet and pulling it over her mother, to warm her, Eilean quietly left the room.

Lunchtime came and her mother stayed in her room. Eilean made herself a peanut butter and jelly sandwich. She thought about toasting it, but decided it was too great a risk. She made one for her mother as well and took it up to her room. She had to push aside a stack of empty pill bottles to make room for the sandwich on the nightstand. It was still sitting there untouched when suppertime came. Eilean turned on the TV and watched cartoons and ate another peanut butter and jelly sandwich, toasted this time. Later, the phone rang and she answered it.

"Hi, honey."

"Hi Daddy. Are you coming home now?"

"I'm at the airport, waiting for a cab. Where's Mommy?"

"She's upstairs."

"Can you go tell her I'm on the phone?"

Eilean put down the receiver and ran upstairs. It was still dark in her mother's room and it looked as if she hadn't moved since Eilean had put the quilt over her that morning. The bread on the nightstand was dry and curling up at the edges. She tried to wake her mother up, but she just lay there. Finally, she gave up and picked up the extension.

"She's still sleeping, Daddy. Maybe she's sick."

There was a pause on the other end.

"Did you hear me, Daddy?"

"Yes, honey. I'll be home real late. But I promise we'll do something special tomorrow, okay?"

"Okay, Daddy."

They spoke for a few more minutes and then he hung up. Eilean looked at her mother, annoyed that she refused to get up. She marched out of the bedroom and got ready for bed. She drew her own bath and brushed her teeth without anyone having to tell her. She went to bed by herself and even turned on the hall light, so that her room wasn't completely dark.

* * *

Eilean had no memory of what happened when her father arrived home. She hadn't the courage to even piece the story together, to imagine what it had been like for him. It was almost fourteen years later and they had never discussed that day. She had asked all kinds of questions about her mother, but they never discussed her death. Eilean knew that he blamed himself for being away too often. And here he was again, flying home, expecting the worst.

"We're here," Ron said. She looked up, a bit startled. She saw that they had arrived at the front gates of Banff National Park. To avoid paying the entrance fee, Ron took the lane on the far right, getting behind trucks and motorhomes just passing through on their way to B.C.

"Any idea where she'd go?"

Eilean nodded. "Chinaman's Gorge."

Ron swore. "That's another half hour at least! Jesus, I hope this isn't a waste of time," he said. Eilean looked out the window, her heart pounding.

Traffic was crazy for early afternoon on a weekday, and Eilean was frightened by some of the near-misses as Ron took chances passing slow-moving vehicles. Finally, they reached the exit to Chinaman's Gorge. Ron honked his horn at a few cars slowing down in the middle of the road, either lost or looking at scenery. He blasted past them as they pulled over to the shoulder. Less than a minute later, they pulled into the parking lot. Without bothering to grab a parking ticket, they ran up the steep stairs leading to the trails. Just as they made it to the bridge that spanned the rushing water at the bottom of the gorge, Eilean spotted something. She grabbed Ron's arm and stopped him, leaning against him for support as she felt the world tilt.

There beneath her, snagged on some tree roots,

was a soaked and tattered backpack. As she watched, a torn fleece jacket floated under the bridge. She knew they were Cathy's.

Chapter 12
Cathy

The sun was shining brightly, burning off the last remaining clouds. Mist from the falls coated her, cool to the skin and beading on her thick black hair. She stood on the narrow shelf and closed her eyes, listening to the roar of the water, birdsong, and the creaking of the ancient trees towering above her.

After a while, she opened her eyes again.

How long have I been standing here?

She saw that the sun had moved in the sky, casting longer shadows along the steep alpine glades high above.

Cathy started to shiver. She was slowly coming back into the world. Jamie had talked about this stage; it was part of his research over the last few months. "It's something Samurais did in Japan, and some Native warriors. All kinds of cultures describe it," he told her excitedly, pointing to the notes he had collected on his laptop computer. He had a whole database in there devoted to only one subject.

"It's like they worked themselves into this state before going into war, preparing for death. If something happened and they didn't die, it took a long time to get back to normal. They were stuck between life and death."

Cathy looked around her at the vast sky, the mountain peaks.

Is that what's happened to me?

Jamie had called her yesterday afternoon. They spoke for only a few minutes, and neither of them had actually said goodbye — but they knew.

Tourists came and went far below her. None of them appeared to see her on her ledge. She had begun to slip out of the trance and experience where she was, soaking in every sound, every sensation. It took her a few moments to realize there was a new sound. It was hard to make it out over the roar of the falls, but she recognized it. Someone was shouting something over and over.

Is it my name?

As the shouting came closer, Cathy recognized the voice. She thought about staying still. Not letting herself be found.

Am I ready for this? Do I really want to come back?

She closed her eyes and knew she had to make up her mind, once and for all.

She listened to the roar, felt it call her voice, but the other voice was louder, more appealing. Cathy turned away from the falls without a final glance.

She looked down at the path on the other side of the high railings and smiled as she saw Eilean run up the final set of stairs, flushed and out of breath.

"Cathy!" Eilean screamed. She called out several more times. Cathy watched as she ran onto the observation deck, looking over the edge into the water. From there, there was no way Eilean would be able to see Cathy. "Oh, Jesus!" she shouted.

"I'm here," Cathy said, her voice sounded calm, and she spoke too softly to be heard. Eilean didn't hear her. Cathy cupped her hands to her mouth and shouted. "I'm here!"

Eilean looked around, trying to place where the voice came from.

"Up here," Cathy shouted, and Eilean saw her this time. Cathy didn't know what to feel when her friend covered her face in her hands and wept. Eilean sank to the the metal deck, sobbing. To Cathy, she looked like a puppet with its strings cut.

Because of me? Is she crying like that over me?

Deep down, something in Cathy began to shift. After a moment, Eilean stood again, reaching out a hand in Cathy's direction.

"Please, Cathy!" Eilean shouted, her voice faraway and childish through the sound of the rushing water. "I want you to come down!"

Cathy nodded and looked for the best way to reach the barrier. She soon discovered that the descent was much tougher than the climb. She scrambled to find footing, and several times nearly lost her grip. The mesh barricade seemed less stable than before, wobbling wildly under her weight. At last she felt her boot hit the solid metal of the railing and she stood on it, using the mesh once more to balance.

As she stepped off the railing back onto the metal deck of the observation area, Cathy slipped. She began to slide over the rail, her fingers slipping on the wet metal, unable to find anything to grip.

Oh my God, she thought, I'm going over after all!

Suddenly, a strong hand gripped her arm, pulling her up and over the railing, tossing her not too gently onto the deck. Shaken by the close call, she looked up at the man who had saved her.

Was that Ron Freis? The bully? Well, whoever it was, he looked pissed.

Eilean rushed over and threw her arms around her friend, hugging her tightly. Cathy wanted to return the hug, and the emotion behind it, but found there was nothing inside her.

Finally Eilean let go and put her hands on Cathy's face, brushing her thick hair from her eyes. Cathy saw Eilean's dirty-blonde hair was wet from the spray.

"Jesus! Are you're okay?"

Cathy didn't know what to say, how to react. She hadn't fully come back to the real world. She could still hear a faint voice urging her back to the waiting falls and to the endless rush of water.

Cathy shook her head to clear it. She tried to

speak, but the words wouldn't come. Eilean stared at her, still holding her face in her hands, staring into her eyes. She had no idea how long they sat there holding each other before Eilean began to calm down. Strangers were walking past, casting them strange looks. She also noticed the tall, dark boy who still waited nearby, looking uncomfortable. He shoved his hands into the pockets of his leather jacket. She thought it was too warm a day for a heavy jacket like that.

"Your name's Ron, right?" Her voice had returned.

He nodded. He was furious, refusing to look at her.

"Ron helped me find you," Eilean said.

Cathy nodded, as if it were a normal thing for Ron Freis to drive Eilean all the way up into the mountains.

"Are you sure you're okay?" Eilean asked. She still looked at Cathy a little warily, held on to her tightly as if she might still throw herself over the falls.

"I think I am," Cathy said. As she spoke, the last of the voices calling her over the edge vanished.

"This is it, right? You're not going to …" Eilean couldn't finish the question. Cathy understood anyway.

"I'm safe." Cathy said.

Eilean nodded and put her arm around her as she led her down the steep stairs and onto the trail.

"I have to tell you something," Eilean said as

they walked. "It's about Sarah and Jamie."

Cathy shook her head. "Please. Don't talk." The reality was just too much for her right now.

They were walking down the stairs, brushing past a group of tourists, and Ron walked ahead. When they reached an open area, Ron turned and stood directly in front of Cathy.

"How do you know?" he said sharply.

"What?" Cathy replied, not sure what he meant. She wondered why he was so angry.

"How do you know about Sarah and the other kid?"

"We all planned it together."

Ron moved closer to her, looming over her, threatening like the bully she had always seen.

"What is wrong with you people?"

"But," she said, wanting to explain, "It was all planned ..."

He cut her off.

"Oh. You had it all planned? That makes it okay?" He swore furiously and turned away, as if not able to stand the sight of her anymore. Cathy looked over at Eilean to see if she knew why he was acting this way. Eilean looked angry too.

"Eilean," Cathy began. "You get it, right?"

Eilean turned slightly away and wrapped her arms tightly about herself.

"I don't want to hear about it. Not now."

"But Eilean ..."

"You heard her! She doesn't want to hear your excuses!"

He'd turned on her again, and Cathy stepped back. It was only from reflex. She was still too numb to feel afraid of him. Eilean stepped between them and pushed Ron back.

"Alright! She's been through enough! She doesn't need a lecture from you!"

Ron glared at Eilean. "That's right! She doesn't need a lecture. She needs someone to slap some sense into her!"

"That's your answer for everything, isn't it Freis? Slap someone around?"

"Why not? That's all some people understand!"

Cathy stepped forward; she didn't want people to argue over her. She put a hand on Ron's arm.

"Jamie was in pain every day. He just wanted peace." She paused and smiled. "And Sarah …"

She stopped when Ron slapped her hand away painfully. The pain seemed to bring her even more back into reality. Eilean was swearing at Ron.

"Don't you touch her! Just leave us alone!"

"Oh, I get it. I was good enough for you when you needed help finding her! You all think you're so special, don't you? You think you're so far above me, you and your little gang. Especially Sarah! You don't even have the guts to face real life!"

"Just get the hell away from us! Leave us alone!"

"Fine. I'll do that!"

He turned away, walking down the path as quickly as he could without actually breaking into a run. Cathy and Eilean watched him until he turned a corner and disappeared beyond an out-cropping of rock.

After a few minutes of silence, Eilean took Cathy's hand.

"Please tell me you drove here," she said.

Cathy nodded. Now all she had to do was remember where she had parked the car.

Chapter 13
Eilean

The whole trip home, Cathy sat silently in the passenger seat, staring straight ahead. Every now and then she would speak, but only to point out something she had seen. Eilean would occasionally steal a glance at her, just making sure Cathy was still breathing and that she didn't unlock the door and jump out in the middle of the highway.

Cathy was pale. She had dark smudges under her eyes and her complexion was blotchy. Just like Sarah. Her black hair was frizzy from the spray.

Maybe Cath's just having a really bad hair day, Eilean thought and smiled.

Eilean sighed and rubbed her aching neck. It was as if all her tension had wedged itself in there.

What a boring trip home. Almost as bad as the trip there. At least this time all the stress was gone. And Cathy was safe.

About half an hour out of Banff she'd grabbed her cell phone to call her dad. She swore, realizing she'd left it on and the battery was dead. She would charge it up as soon as she got Cathy safely home.

As she reached Cathy's street, Eilean slowed the car.

"Stop," Cathy said.

Eilean looked at Cathy, surprised to hear her speak. What now?

"Why?"

"I can't do it."

Eilean nodded and pulled over to the side. She put the car in neutral and looked over at Cathy, waiting. They were less than half a block away and Cathy's house was clearly visible. Eilean noticed that Cathy wouldn't look at it.

What was going on in her mind?

When she spoke again, there was no emotion in her voice.

"What'll I say?"

"Just tell them what happened."

"Are you crazy? My mom will kill me."

What a bizarre thing to say. Eilean almost smiled at the seriousness of Cathy's tone. Didn't she hear what she'd just said? Still, she did have a point. Her mom could get a little extreme. She'd gone nuts on Cathy for far less than this.

"She might be mad. But mostly I think she'll be glad you're okay."

"She'll lose it over this. She'll be embarrassed more than anything. And worried her friends'll find out."

Eilean shook her head. "You know your mom loves you. And she needs to know you're okay. I saw her this morning, remember? She was freaking. And she needs to get you help."

Cathy looked at her for the first time. Eilean noticed there was no expression in her eyes.

"Help with what? It's all over."

Eilean said nothing, but thought: Yeah, sure it is. I know next to nothing about psychiatry, but I'm pretty sure this ain't over.

She had seen the look in Cathy's eyes up at the gorge. Cathy wasn't all the way back even now. She was still in some cold and unhappy place. They just sat there for a moment, not saying a word, and then Eilean tried again.

"We all have to go home sometime."

Cathy didn't seem to hear her, lost as she was in her own thoughts. Eilean waited as long as she could.

"Okay," she said finally. "What do you want? Just tell me and I'll do it."

"Let's go to Sarah's. She'll know what to do."

Eilean was stunned. And then she saw the colour drain from Cathy's cheeks as she realized what she'd just said.

"I forgot! How could I forget?" She burst into tears and reached to for Eilean. Eilean held her friend close, stroking her hair, rocking her gently as she cried. She felt her own tears fall. Sarah wasn't there for them. She might never be again. Cathy shook in her arms, and Eilean felt a strange relief.

"It's okay, Cath," she said. "Let it all out."

After a few minutes the sobbing slowed and Cathy leaned back against her seat.

"You must hate me. After everything I've done."

Eilean felt the tears come again. For some reason, this hurt her even more than the thought of Sarah.

"Oh, God, no!" Eilean cried. "Don't even think that. You're my friend! Nothing will change that."

They held each other for a long time and then sat back again. Both looked at each other sheepishly, embarrassed by their emotions.

Cathy looked back at her house. Eilean thought she was deciding to go home at last. But Cathy had other thoughts.

"The poor parents," she said. "They must be totally destroyed."

Eilean nodded. "That's why we have to get you home."

What were they going through? Eilean couldn't even blame Sarah's mom for how angry she'd been, how she'd lashed out.

Eilean put the car into drive and pulled out, stopping at the bottom of Cathy's driveway.

"I can't!" Cathy said, crying once more. "I just can't face them!"

For a moment, Eilean felt a rush of rage. She had the impulse to grab Cathy by the collar and drag her into her house.

It had been a long, long day, and Eilean didn't know how much more she could take.

The feeling passed as quickly as it had come, leaving her feeling confused and guilty. She did her best to sound calm.

"You have to see someone. I'm not letting you out of my sight until then!"

Cathy nodded.

"There are counsellors at school. Do you want to go there?"

"School," she said. "Someone at school."

Eilean nodded and put the car in gear. She inched forward, picking up speed slowly, turned left at the next intersection, heading for school. As she drove, she remembered that counsellors from the school board were supposed to be in the neighbourhood. They would be in places where students hung out.

The school was coming up on the right, but Eilean turned sharply left, toward the small strip mall that bordered the school property.

"Where are we going?" Cathy asked.

"For coffee."

Eilean parked in front of the VitalBean. She tried not to think of her date to skip class and have a latte here with Sarah that morning. A white Ford Focus with the Calgary Board of Education logo on the door was parked nearest the door. Eilean shut off the engine and turned to Cathy.

"Don't get out until I come around." It was clearly an order and Cathy nodded, staying put. She opened the passenger door, grabbed Cathy by the arm and escorted her inside. It was busy, but not nearly as busy as it usually was.

The smells nearly made her stop. Cinnamon and spices, dark coffee, pastries.

She'd been in here a hundred times. All those skipped classes, all the early mornings and late nights after a movie or a party. She and Sarah would sit here and talk about boys or music or anything else that was important to them.

I'll never feel that way again here.

There were booths at the front and Eilean saw a pleasant-looking woman sitting in the middle one, facing two girls who were thirteen or fourteen. The woman had a large coffee cup, untouched, and a cell phone sitting at her elbow. A small notebook was on the other side, a pen sitting on top. No way that wasn't a counsellor. Eilean pulled Cathy along toward the booth. The woman looked up at them.

"We need to talk to you."

"Of course. I'm almost finished here, and then we …"

Eilean pulled Cathy forward. "This is Cathy Chen and she tried to kill herself today." The woman looked momentarily stunned, then nodded soberly.

Kids nearby turned to look. The two girls jumped up, slipping from the booth. They stared at Cathy as they walked past. Eilean stared them down, waiting, daring them to say anything, anything at all.

The girls were silent as they left the shop.

"Well, please sit down."

The woman indicated the now vacant seat. Eilean let Cathy into the booth first, and sat beside her to block her escape. Just in case. The woman glanced at her notebook, and Eilean knew she was checking a list of names written there.

"And who are you?" the woman asked, pleasantly.

"Eilean Mull," she replied. "I'm in your book."

The woman smiled and didn't look at the book.

"I'm glad you came to see me," she said. "Both of you."

"Before we start, can I use your phone?" Eilean asked, remembering her own useless one sitting in her purse. The woman hesitated.

"It's to call my dad," Eilean added. "He's probably worried about me."

The woman nodded and handed her the phone. Eilean slid around, facing away from them as she dialed. She held the phone to her left ear, her hand blocking the other one as the phone rang. It seemed to ring forever until it finally connected and she heard a familiar voice answer.

"Dad!" she said, tears falling. "It's me! I'm okay, Dad." She paused, and then added, "I'm safe."

Chapter 14
Ron

Ron sat in his room, picking at the strings of his guitar, occasionally pacing or sorting through his CDs, unable to concentrate on anything.

What now? What the hell could he do now?

The whole day had sucked, really. All the crap that happened, the assembly, the crazy drive up to the mountains, the even crazier chick they'd gone there to get. And then that Eilean screamed at him, like *he* was the psycho! All he wanted was to help her out. Look where that got him.

Well screw her! Screw all of them! His dad was right, that's what happened when you were weak, when you tried to help people! Dear old Dad, he was as predictable as ever. He'd been waiting in the foyer when Ron made it home. Of course the school had called him at his office, of course Ron was in deep trouble, and, of course he was grounded yet again.

His farther had nearly shouted himself hoarse.

On and on. Blah, blah, blah. Like Ron hadn't heard all the threats a million times.

Ron had walked directly to his room at the first pause in his father's rant, and he planned on staying there for as long as he could. He leaned against the window, looking out.

Man, he was so tired. Tired of it all. Tired of his parents, of school, of all the stupid rules everyone tried to force down his throat. Tired of his stupid friends and all the immature games they played.

What was the point of any of it? He couldn't honestly say he knew.

I'm tired of my life.

Ron walked over to his computer desk and opened the case that held his CDs. Stuffed tightly at the back was an envelope from a one-hour photo place. He slipped the prints out and sat on the edge of his bed as he leafed through them. They were taken last summer, at an overnight camping party up at Ghost River. There were several shots of his drunken friends, posing for the camera. Near the back were the ones he needed to see, the ones of him and Sarah. He looked at the last photograph, her sitting on his lap wearing a bathing suit, her white-blonde hair washed out by the camera flash. She had the strangest expression as she stared back into the camera

Was it a smile? He had no idea. No real surprise there. Nobody could figure out Sarah's moods.

There was a loud knock, and he shoved the pictures under his quilt as the door swung open. His father stood there, his tie knotted tightly at his throat, his suit jacket folded carefully over his right arm.

"We're leaving for the club now," his father said. "Don't even think about leaving this house tonight. Understood?"

Ron shrugged and turned away. After a final stare, his father shut the door. Ron waited until he heard the sound of the garage door closing a few moments later as his parents drove away. He looked at the photos one more time and swore.

"What's wrong with me? I'm sulking like a girl!" he shouted to the empty room. Ron tossed the pile of photographs across the room; they hit the wall and then fluttered behind his computer monitor.

He needed a drink! It was becoming a habit.

He ran down the stairs, turning left into the hall, through the kitchen toward the rear of the house and his father's den. The door was always locked, but he'd gotten good at opening doors.

"Welcome to The Armoury, folks," he said, turning to an imaginary tour group. It was something he did often as he wandered the halls of his parents' house alone. "Follow me. Please don't touch any of the exhibits and no flash photography is allowed."

He stepped inside, not bothering to turn on a light, heading for the wet bar behind his father's antique desk. A shelf over the bar held a wide assortment of liquor. He grabbed a crystal decanter of single malt scotch, turned over a matching crystal tumbler, filled it nearly to the top, and took a deep gulp.

That's the ticket, he thought, feeling the whisky burn as it slid down his throat. He coughed.

God! He could barely breathe! Who could ever get used to the taste?

Ron dropped into the deep leather chair, threw a leg over one overstuffed arm and took another sip. It didn't burn quite so badly this time.

"Third time's a charm," he said, saluting the empty room. "Whatever the hell that means!" He tossed back the rest of the scotch, and then rolled the cool crystal of the empty tumbler against his forehead for a moment. Ron started spinning the chair wildly. Light spilled in from the hallway, showing some details of the room.

Spin

He saw shelves of law books, pictures in expensive mountings.

Spin

He saw trophies and awards, stuffed animal heads from his grandfather's day.

Spin

He stopped the chair and looked at the wall to the right of the desk. There he saw the glass-covered display case that held his father's collection of antique firearms. Beside them was a thick metal gun cabinet, over two metres high. These were why the room was called "The Armoury."

Ron stood and poured another full glass of scotch.

He took a sip and shifted the tumbler to his left hand while his right fumbled under the top of the desk. A small drawer popped open and he took out the keys inside. He sipped his drink before placing it on the desk, right on top of an open file. A little scotch sloshed out onto his father's work, something that would normally be a disaster; but Ron didn't care.

Ron walked over to the gun cabinet and unlocked it. There was a thick lever on the face that he needed two hands to pull down. He heard a click, and the door, nearly eight inches of steel, swung open on well-oiled hinges. A light came on, highlighting the gleaming weapons racked inside.

Ron had loved being in this room as a boy, sneaking in when his father was out or away on business. He touched the cool metal of a pair of matching shotguns. They had been his grandfather's. One of them was the one that had killed him in that hunting accident. Ron had always wondered which.

One more useless death. And stupid. Just like those friends of Sarah's.

He thought again about the day, about the frantic search for Cathy, about the skinny little kid who killed himself. He thought about Eilean, how he had left her in the mountains. And then he thought about Sarah.

Sarah. Why did you do it? Why did you dump me like that?

He remembered their wild summer together, and no matter how hard he tried, he could find no clue as to why she had dumped him once school started.

No apology, no nothing. Like she was ashamed people would find out about them.

Ron picked up his drink, took a gulp.

One memory in particular kept returning. The night that they had all decided to break into school, weeks before classes were to begin again. It had started as a joke, but Sarah had become excited at the idea. It was she who had pushed them on. Ron and his gang had broken into places before, mostly when they were younger, stealing a few things, messing the place up. They had never done anything as big as breaking into school. That night, he showed Sarah how to open a locked door.

That must have been how Sarah got into Klein's office.

He took another gulp of scotch.

The phone rang on his father's desk. Ron ignored it, assuming it wasn't for him. It continued to ring so he glanced at the call display screen, surprised when he saw who was calling. He grabbed the receiver as he sat in the chair.

"Hello?"

"Ron?"

"Yeah?"

"It's Eilean."

"I know. And?"

He was glad she had called, but couldn't bring himself to act like it.

"Look, I just wanted to say I was sorry about this afternoon. I shouldn't have acted that way."

He wanted to tell her off for treating him like

that. He wanted to tell her what he thought of her and her stupid friends. He sighed and took a sip of scotch.

"Forget it. It's been a pretty weird day for everyone."

There was a long pause. He told himself: She's going to hang up. Think, stupid! Talk to her. Tell her what you're feeling for Christ's sake!"

"Well …" Eilean began.

"So this friend, Cathy," he said quickly. "What happened with her?"

"I took her to a counsellor. She called her parents and they took her to hospital for observation."

"Did they freak? Her parents?"

"You could say that," Eilean said. There was another pause.

"I better get going. I want to call the hospital again. See how Sarah's doing."

Ron felt the now familiar lurch in his gut at the mention of her name. He sat forward, elbows resting on the green blotter on the desktop as he finished the scotch. Once again, he rubbed the cool crystal against his forehead.

"You wanna try to see her? I could drive."

There was a pause.

"Thanks," she finally said. "But they're still only letting family in."

He needed her to stay on the line. Just one more minute.

"Eilean?" he managed to say.

"Yes?"

"I need to talk about Sarah."

The pause was much longer this time.

"What about her?"

"Look, could you come over here? I can't tell you over the phone."

"We could meet somewhere I guess," she said.

"My parents grounded me, actually. I gotta stay in. I really need to talk."

Grounded. That sounded pretty lame. Well, it wasn't like he hadn't been grounded a million times before. Like it even mattered anyway.

"I don't know. My dad's home now. I doubt if he'll even let me go out tonight."

"Try, okay? I need to tell you what happened."

"I don't get what you mean."

"Just come over, okay?"

"I'll see." She hung up.

Ron sat in his father's chair for a few moments before replacing the receiver. He stood and poured himself another scotch.

Chapter 15
Eilean

Eilean sat across the table from her dad. He hadn't changed out of the heavy work clothes he wore on the oilfields. He hadn't even taken off his coat. She had always thought she looked more like him than her mom. They had the same lifeless hair, the same green eyes.

He looked tired. And worried.

She saw that he hadn't shaved for days, and there was a lot of grey in the stubble.

They sat in the breakfast nook talking, only stopping while she made them coffee and sandwiches. It took a while for her to convince him she was okay, that he never had to worry about her trying to kill herself.

Like the idea had ever occurred to me. I'm nothing like my mom. I don't even know about her, not really.

There were a few things Eilean did know for sure. Her mom played the guitar and Eilean never took a lesson. Her mom majored in English in college. Eilean liked science. Her mom kept the house spotless. Eilean only cleaned when she had to. Her mom wandered around, crying all the time.

Eilean stopped.

She'd been terribly lonely since she and the other three had drifted apart, even when her dad was at home. Eilean just shut herself in her room, listening to music, reading poems.

Yeah, not to mention crying for no reason and not being able to stop!

It was a minor glitch. She'd get over herself. She was, after all, Eilean: the island.

She smiled, remembering when she was twelve or thirteen and she picked up one of those cheap little books at the supermarket. This one had a picture of an unattractive baby on the cover and was titled, *Baby Names and Their Origins*. The first name she looked up was her own. Her name was Gaelic and meant, "Island."

How did her parents know when they named her?

All her life Eilean had kept herself slightly apart from others, even her close friends.

That's why she was so amazed by the way Sarah used to fit into any crowd and could charm anyone.

The coffee was finished and Eilean saw that it was past nine o'clock. She stood and cleared the table.

"Are you sure you have to go out?" her dad asked, following her to the front door.

"I have a friend who needs to talk."

Her dad nodded and handed her the keys to his car. She kissed his cheek and said goodnight. He hugged her tight, holding her as if afraid to let her go. A few minutes later, Eilean pulled up to a gatehouse and rolled down the car window. The uniformed guard leaned out. He looked bored

"Can I help you?" he asked.

"Eilean Mull to see Ron Freis," she said. The guard looked at a computer screen and then nodded. The gates swung open and Eilean drove up the steep driveway into the gated community. To say she was amazed would be a bit of an understatement. Here she was at the top of Nose Hill, driving past houses that looked like small hotels, searching for Ron's house. How could a guy who dressed like Ron live here? She found the house at the far end of a cul-de-sac, sitting apart from the others, an imposing brick building that could easily have been an English country estate. She drove up the curving driveway, past the rock pool and the six-car garage, and parked near the front entrance. Ron was waiting at the top of a short set of steps.

"Nice place you have," she said.

Ron darkened slightly.

"It's not mine," he replied. "It's my dad's. Come on in."

He stepped aside and she walked through the high doors and into a massive foyer. The first thing she saw was a double staircase leading upstairs, past a huge crystal chandelier. There were six doors in the foyer that she supposed lead to different rooms. The place was a museum, not a house.

"You want a drink?" he said.

She turned to look at Ron, and she saw that he'd been drinking. His eyes were red and a little droopy, and even at this distance she could smell the booze on his breath.

"Maybe a Coke."

"Come on, my folks are out! You can have something a bit better than that."

"Coke's fine," she said a little coolly.

He shrugged. "Let's go to the kitchen, and I'll give you a quick tour."

She followed him through a set of tall doors and down a wide hall into an enormous kitchen and dining area, complete with vaulted ceilings. She could see the evening sky through cut-glass windows high in the far walls. The kitchen looked like the set of TV cooking show, marble and stainless steel being the dominant features. Ron opened the door of one of the refrigerators and pulled out a can of Coke. He poured it into a glass and handed it to her. She took it and he gestured, indicating she should follow.

The tour began in the dining room, passing into the Great Room, a glassed-in sunroom, and finally into a darkly panelled room with a huge desk and leather chair at the far end. Eilean's eyes locked on a large assortment of guns mounted in cases that took up an entire wall. A huge metal safe was beside them, it's thick door wide open. It too was filled with guns. Eilean looked at it, worried.

"Should that thing be open?"

"This is my father's little collection," Ron said.
Eilean nodded. "He likes guns, huh?"

"Ya think?" Ron said, laughing a bit too hard.

He walked along the wall, his hand gently
brushing the glass of the cabinets.

"Some of the guns here are over two hundred
years old."

"That's nice," she said. She looked around at
the dark room, saw the books and the trophies, the
animal heads hung above them, thinking: This is
creepy. What kind of person thinks this looks
good?

She tried not to look at the guns, feeling extremely
uncomfortable around them. And around Ron. He
stood a little too close.

"You want to see upstairs?" he asked.

"That's okay," she said quickly. "You wanted to
talk about Sarah."

"So I did. Let me get myself a drink and then
we'll head for the living room."

He walked behind the desk and poured a drink
from a decanter. He turned back and raised his
glass in salute before taking a gulp. He started to
choke a little, laughing, eyes tearing.

"Good stuff, huh?" she said, watching him.

"The best." His breathing was back under control. She followed him into one of the huge rooms
where matching sofas faced each other in front of
a fireplace high enough to walk into. Above it was
a large family portrait in an overly elaborate

frame. It was taken when Ron was thirteen or so, and he looked nervous between his parents. She saw immediately Ron's resemblance to his father.

It's kind of ugly, she thought, compared to the way the rest of the room was decorated.

Eilean sat on one of the sofas, and Ron sat on the floor, leaning against the opposite sofa. He watched her examine the portrait and then held up his glass, saluting it.

"The rest of the place was decorated by my mom. The Armoury and that picture are dad's contribution. He wanted to show everyone we're one big happy family, dammit!"

Ron laughed and sipped his drink. He paused for a moment as if thinking something over, staring at the carpet.

Here we go, Eilean thought, time for Ron to get serious.

"Sarah never talked to you about me? Or what happened last summer?"

"No."

Ron shook his head. He sat up a bit and rubbed his face hard, trying to shake the effects of the liquor. "I can't believe her!"

"So what happened last summer?"

"Sarah and I spent it together."

Well, Eilean thought, that explains a lot. No wonder she didn't bother with me.

"Tell me about it," she said.

Ron didn't need encouragement. He opened right up. He told her about how they'd met, her wild behaviour, the sudden mood swings, her need to try new things, to keep getting wilder.

"I gotta tell you," Ron said after more than half an hour of talking, "things got intense. She wanted to do stuff I thought was nuts."

"So what'd you do?"

"Anything she told me," he said, laughing.

"Like what?"

"Stupid stuff, crazy stuff. Speeding up and down McLeod Trail. Drugs. Breaking into school."

"That was you? And Sarah?"

"It was her idea."

His glass was empty now. He looked sadly at the carpet, shaking his head. He traced its pattern with a finger as he spoke again.

"Then school starts and bam!" He hit the plush carpet with the palm of his hand. "That was it! She wouldn't talk to me, wouldn't even look at me!" Ron swore and rubbed his eyes, looking away from her as if trying to keep from crying.

"She didn't talk to you at all after that?" she asked. He shook his head.

"Then you don't know what happened to her?"

"What happened to her?" Ron asked, his eyes finally meeting hers.

"She got pregnant."

The colour left Ron's face. He looked as if someone had hit him in the stomach. Eilean placed her drink carefully on the glass end table.

"Is it all true? You're really the guy she was with last summer?"

He nodded.

"Okay," she said. "This is what happened."

* * *

That fall, Sarah's behaviour kept getting worse. No one had seen much of her all summer and when she arrived at school in September, they were all shocked at her appearance. She had always been thin, but a healthy thin. Now she was like a skeleton. Her skin was pasty, and there were deep shadows under her eyes. She barely spoke during the first few days, like she was zoned all the time. After about three weeks of this, she suddenly showed up looking happy and alert, with that weird shine in her eyes telling you she was in her intense mood. She hung out with Eilean and the others again. Jamie and Cathy were so relieved she was back, they barely questioned her horrible behaviour.

She told them a little about her summer, about some of the wild parties, but when asked for details, she was pretty vague. Eilean was tougher on her than the others, letting Sarah know she didn't take her stories too seriously. Then one day at lunch she pulled out a small vial of pills.

"Anyone want desert?" she said, grinning. She opened the vial and shook a few of the tablets into her palm. "You guys have gotta try these! You'll feel great for hours!"

Eilean and the others were disgusted. Not just

because she had drugs, but because she was also showing them in the middle of a crowded lunch-room.

"What are you doing!" Eilean whispered. "Get rid of those!"

Sarah shrugged. "Okay," she said, and swallowed one. She tossed the pills back in the vial.

"Sarah!" Jamie said. "Are you crazy?"

"Oh please! Stop being such a girl!"

Jamie blushed.

"See ya later, losers."

She dropped the vial in her purse and stood, walking quickly away from the table. The three of them just stared at each other, shocked.

"Why is she acting this way?" Cathy asked, looking worried.

"I don't know," Eilean replied.

"Come on," Jamie said, always her defender. "It's just Sarah being Sarah. You know, wanting to shock us. Shake you up a bit. Those were probably candies."

"They looked pretty real to me," Cathy said.

"Like you're the expert on drugs?" Jamie said, giving her arm a gentle push. She brushed him away, annoyed.

Sarah went downhill from there. She talked back to teachers, disrupted classes by trying to be funny. Eilean was never sure if she was just acting up, or if she was on something. Either way, no one was amused. Early one morning, just before home room, Eilean ran into Sarah in the washroom. She was leaning over a sink, rinsing her mouth and looking a little queasy.

"What's the matter?"

"Not much," Sarah said. She stood up, checked her reflection in the mirror, threw her purse over her shoulder and headed for the door. As she opened it, she turned back to Eilean, that same hyper look in her eye.

"I'm just knocked up."

With that, she casually stepped outside. Eilean ran into the hall after her, but Sarah was already walking into her first class. Sarah avoided her the rest of the morning. Eilean waited at the usual table at lunch. Jamie arrived first.

"Have you seen Sarah?"

"Yeah, she went home"

Eilean grabbed her cell and called Sarah's. There was no answer.

"What's up?" Jamie asked.

"Nothing. I just need to talk to her." This felt too personal to let Jamie in on.

That night she called Sarah at home. Her mom answered.

"Sarah's lying down. She's not feeling well."

"Did she say what was wrong?" Eilean asked.

"Not really. It's probably one of those twenty-four hour things."

Eilean hesitated before asking the next question.

"Has Sarah been acting a bit strange lately?"

"Well, we all know Sarah likes attention."

Eilean wanted to say that what was happening with Sarah was a bit more than that. She didn't bother. Sarah's mother believed all kinds of New Age stuff about raising a child. Even Sarah had got sick of it once in a while, wanting her to act more like a normal mom.

Eilean wondered how a normal mom acted.

"Could you ask her to call me?"

"Sure. Where have you been lately? We never see you anymore."

"Just busy with school and junk," Eilean said, hanging up as soon as she could.

As usual, her father was out of town, but he always called at night to make sure she was all right. That evening, he sensed immediately that something was wrong. After a moment's debate, she decided to tell him what had happened at school.

"What should I do, Dad?" she had asked. "She won't talk to me about it."

"You have to talk to her. Tell her she needs help."

"That won't be easy. You know Sarah."

"Are you sure her parents don't know?"

"It doesn't seem like it."

"Then you should tell them."

"What? I can't! I can't go behind Sarah's back like that!"

"If she's taking drugs, and if she really is pregnant, her parents have to be told."

"I know."

"If you want, I could go with you. I could cut the trip short."

"Thanks, Dad. I need to think first."

"Just don't take too long."

There was a pause. "Listen," he said. "This is just Sarah, right? You're not into …"

"Oh, please, Dad!"

"Promise me, Eilean. You'll be careful."

"I promise."

After he hung up, she sat in the breakfast nook trying to figure out what to do.

I can't rat out Sarah, Eilean thought. She's been my best friend forever.

Over the next few days, she tried to talk to her. Sarah just laughed the whole thing off, ignoring her. That was when Eilean made her biggest mistake. She decided to seek the advice of the school counsellor, Miss Klein. They met in Klein's office, a week or so after Sarah's announcement in the girl's washroom. Klein listened patiently, occasionally making notes as Eilean told her all about Sarah's erratic behaviour and that she might be pregnant. Klein only looked up when Eilean told her about the drugs.

"I see," Klein said at last. "Are you sure she's used drugs on school property?"

"I've seen her. More than once."

Klein nodded and stood.

"I'm glad you came to me. Sarah's lucky to have a friend like you." Eilean stood as well, knowing that the meeting was over.

"Nothing's going to happen to her, right? She

won't get into trouble? She just needs help."

"I'll do what has to be done. Trust me," Klein said.

Less than an hour later, all hell broke loose.

Eilean and Sarah were in Social Studies when the principal arrived with a security guard and asked Sarah to follow him. The police had been called to force Sarah's locker open and they found her drugs. Eilean rushed upstairs to the admin offices, and found Klein waiting outside the principal's door.

"What did you do?" Eilean screamed at her. Klein just stood there, looking calmly at Eilean.

"I told you so you could help Sarah, not have the school come down on her like this!" She had never been this angry at a teacher before. Never felt so betrayed by anyone.

"Eilean," Klein said at last. "You are perfectly aware of Calf Robe's zero tolerance on drugs. It's out of our hands now. The police will handle it from here."

"The police?!" Eilean had screamed. "I told you this in private. You promised you'd help Sarah ..."

Klein cut her off. "Miss Mull! We are helping Sarah. You're old enough to know I can't let her continue this behaviour. You may feel you're already an adult, but in the eyes of the law, you're both still children." Klein actually smiled then. "It seems harsh right now, I know. One day you'll understand why we had to do this."

Eilean was too angry to think. Sarah was her

141

friend, and Eilean had betrayed her. Miss Klein entered Powers' office and Eilean caught a brief glimpse of Sarah, a police officer standing beside her. Just before the door closed, their eyes met. Eilean was sure that Sarah knew who had done this to her.

Sarah disappeared from school immediately after. When Eilean tried to call Sarah's home, no one picked up. A few nights later, Eilean was jarred awake by her phone ringing. She picked it up, still half asleep.

"Eilean?" Sarah's voice on the other end was weak and frightened.

"Sarah?" Eilean sat up, fully awake now. She glanced at her call display and saw that the call was from a blocked number. "What's going on?"

"I lost it, Eilean," Sarah said, her voice barely audible.

"You lost what?" Eilean blurted out without thinking. Then she knew what Sarah had meant. "Where are you?"

"I was bleeding, and it hurt so much, Eilean."

"Are you okay now? Are you safe?"

There was a pause. "I'm at the hospital. Please come. I need to see you."

It took a few tries, but Eilean finally managed to get Sarah to tell her which hospital. She dressed quickly and called a cab. When it arrived less than twenty minutes later, she grabbed her things and a handful of cash from the emergency stash her father always left. At the hospital, Sarah's father was asleep in a chair outside. Her mother sat beside him, staring out the window. She turned when she saw Eilean and looked a little surprised.

"Sarah called me," Eilean said and Sarah's mother nodded. "How is she?"

"She's stable now," she said. "The doctors said she'll be fine in a few days."

"And she lost the baby?"

"The baby?" her mother had said. "She told you that nonsense, too? You know Sarah better than that! She's a good girl! The doctors are running tests to see what caused all this."

Eilean wondered who needed help the most, Sarah or her mother. Did she really want Sarah to be seriously ill? Was that better than knowing she was pregnant?

"One thing before I let you go in," Sarah's mother said, stepping in front of the door.

Before you *let* me? Eileen thought. What makes you think I'd let you stop me.

"I don't want you to mention this pregnancy nonsense. We're not playing along with her. Understand?"

For a moment, Eilean was speechless.

"I'm going to check on her," she finally said and pushed past her. "She needs me."

Sarah was awake when Eilean walked up to the bed and held her, both of them sobbing.

"I'm so sorry," Eilean said. "About everything!" Sarah nodded and kept on sobbing. They sat together holding hands until a nurse came to ask Eilean to let Sarah rest. Sarah never mentioned who the father had been.

It took nearly a month, but her parents pulled strings and Sarah was eventually allowed back in school. Eilean didn't know what the terms were, but she knew that Sarah was forced into some kind of program. She and Sarah were fine about what had happened between them. But the rest of her class treated her like a traitor. Cathy and Jamie were cold as well, even though they knew Sarah had needed some kind of help. As far as Eilean knew, Sarah never told anyone else about the pregnancy.

* * *

"That's when her obsession with death and that morbid stuff began," Eilean said.

Ron had hardly moved since she began to tell the story. He looked almost sick.

Eilean decided not to tell him about Sarah's hysterical calls that she had received in the middle of the night. She couldn't tell him about Sarah's nightmares of carrying something dead inside her, her fear that she was diseased and could never have a baby again. Eilean didn't want to tell him how Sarah was fixated on Klein, blamed her for the miscarriage. The only good thing was Sarah blamed Klein and not her for what had happened. Sarah showed her some of the disgusting e-mails and faxes she sent Klein, filled with threats and pictures of dead babies. She sent them anonymously of course, but Klein had to know.

Ron shook his head and then wiped his eyes.

"I would've helped her if she'd told me."

"I know," Eilean found herself saying.

"I could have done something. Maybe she wouldn't have tried to kill herself."

He buried his face in his hands and she saw his shoulders shake as the pain overcame him. He seemed so helpless. Eilean hesitated at first, but finally she stood and walked over to him, tentatively putting an arm across his shoulders. He turned and threw his arms around her, and almost as a reflex, the way she would do with anyone. Eilean started to stroke his hair, to comfort him. After a while he looked up at her, and she stroked his tear-streaked face, impulsively kissing him on the cheek.

He started to kiss her back, holding her tightly.

"That's enough, Ron," she said. He didn't stop. "You're drunk, Stop it!"

He kept kissing her, his hands gripping her tightly. She struggled with him, finally managing to free her right arm and then hitting him in the face. She screamed again for him to let her go. Finally he did, moving away from her, dazed.

"I'm so sorry," he said. "I don't know what got into me." Then he took a step toward her, reaching out to her.

"Please, don't go. I won't ..."

"Stay away from me!" He ignored her and stumbled closer. She slapped him and stepped back, grabbing her things. "I was trying to help you! I was trying to be nice! You're so disgusting!"

With that, she turned and ran out the front door to her car. She didn't see as Ron stumbled after her and fell. She heard a noise behind her, like glass breaking. Eilean kept going.

Chapter 16
Ron

Ron pushed himself to his feet and only then noticed the ragged gash on his left wrist. Blood dripped from his fingers, staining the thick woven carpet. He had stumbled chasing Eilean and had fallen onto the glass-covered coffee table, shattering it. He looked around for something to bind the wound and, seeing nothing, took off his T-shirt and wrapped it tightly around his wrist. Blood soaked through almost immediately. Ron didn't notice. He looked down at the damage and wondered if he should clean it up. After a few seconds he turned away, deciding it wasn't worth the effort. He would catch hell whether he cleaned it up or not.

Cradling the injured arm against his chest, he walked back to The Armoury. He stumbled a little as he passed the desk, his thigh hitting the edge sharply. He ignored the pain and grabbed a fresh glass, filling it with scotch. Ron took a long gulp and fell into the deep leather chair. He took another drink and his thoughts drifted to the dead boy, to all the times he'd tormented him, called him those awful names.

"Eilean's right," he said aloud. "I am disgusting. I don't know how to act like a normal person."

He sat in silence for a moment before reaching into the back pocket of his jeans. He took out the bent photograph he had stuffed there earlier, the one of Sarah sitting on his lap last summer.

"I miss you, Spook," he said quietly, then smiled at the stupid name he and his friends had called her. It suited Sarah so well.

Ron sat forward, elbows on the desk, forgetting the shirt wrapped around his wrist. It fell onto a stack of papers.

"I thought about going over to you a million times at school," he said to the image in the photograph. "Making you talk to me, making you tell me what happened."

Ron remembered the imagined conversation he had played over and over in his mind. He saw Spook leaning against her locker, looking up at him and smiling, her arms crossed casually over her stomach.

"So what's it going to be?" he would say. "We getting back together or what?" He would have to sound tough. He knew she liked him best when he took charge.

Maybe, she'd say.

"There's no maybe. Are we or aren't we?"

She would grin and push him away from the locker, and he would get annoyed by her coy act.

Maybe, she'd say again. Then she would walk down the hall.

Meet me after school, she would say.

And he would grin because that meant they were on again. She'd forgiven him for whatever he'd done wrong.

He took a sip of scotch and closed his eyes, feeling a little sleepy. His head snapped forward and he was awake again. Ron could feel Spook's presence in the room, sitting in the shadows just out of sight. He knew that if he squinted a little, he would just make her out. Ron felt a tickle on his left wrist and rubbed his arm against his jeans, barely registering that the gash was still bleeding.

"I would have helped, if only you'd told me," he said softly to his unseen Spook.

"That's what a man would do," Ron said. "That's how I was raised. A man would stand with you. Take care of you!"

That's what a man would do alright, Spook replied.

"Man! That was a summer we had! Remember how wild we got? You were the craziest person I ever met." He grinned at the memory. Spook had to smile as well. "We'd be great together for weeks, then you'd start to get all weird. And then you were gone!"

"I never told anyone," he said. "But you kind of scared me. I mean, I've never been scared of anything in my life, right? But you scared me. You made me see I wasn't as tough as I thought.

"Fritz was the one that came up with your nickname. Because you were all white and pale, always disappearing. Like a ghost."

"Old Fritz really wanted you, too. It was the first time a chick came between us."

He was pretty obvious, Spook said, and Ron sat forward.

"Did he try something?" Spook didn't answer. Ron swore. "I'm definitely going to have words with him!"

Ron drained the glass. He stood up shakily and poured himself another, not noticing that some of the scotch spilled over the glass and into the carpet. He started to wander the room, talking out loud as Spook sat still, listening.

"Sarah Spokes," he said. "Sarah Spooks. Spook."

Spook laughed. I never had a nickname before, she said.

"Why did you dump me, Spook?" he asked at last.

Because I didn't need you anymore.

He cheered up, noticing the guns, thousands of dollars hanging behind thick glass panels and racked in the metal gun safe. "What do you think of the collection, Spook? Pretty cool, huh?"

If you say so, she said.

Ron set his drink on the wet bar and walked over to the gun safe. He pulled out one of the matched shotguns, handling it carefully as he brought it over to the desk and sat down. He worked the mechanism a few times and dry fired the gun.

"These are over a hundred years old!" he said. "Dad's pride and joy. A matched set of double-barrelled Holland and Holland shotguns. They cost more than his car!"

Impressive, Spook said, not sounding the least bit impressed.

Her attitude was starting to annoy him. He stood, walked over to the cabinet and opened a drawer. He fumbled with the heavy shotgun as he reached inside to remove a box of shells. He cracked open the breech and placed a shell in each barrel.

What are you up to? Spook asked calmly.

Ron didn't answer as he snapped the breech shut and held out the gun, admiring it. He ran his fingers over the elaborate scrollwork etched into the barrel, touched the stock made of beautifully worked walnut.

"He would spend hours cleaning and polishing these. When I was really young, I was jealous of them!" he laughed. "Can you believe that? Jealous because my old man spent more time with his freaking guns than with me!"

Ron felt light-headed, the room spun. He fell forward and put a hand out to grab the desk.

Steady there, cowboy, Spook said.

"Whoo! That was a rush!" he said, shaking his head. He stumbled behind the desk again and sat down.

He stayed there for a while, half nodding off. He thought of the skinny boy again (what was his name? Jimmy? Jamie?), dead now. He remembered tormenting him, slamming his skinny little body into a locker, and now that body was stone cold, lifeless. Ron thought about the Asian girl they'd found up in the mountains, the stunned look on her face.

And he thought about Sarah, lying in a coma in a hospital.

But Spook was fine. They were together again, like it was supposed to be.

"How could life be so bad that they wanted to kill themselves?" he asked. "What is the attraction?" He placed the butt of the shotgun on the floor and cocked the hammers. Ron placed his forehead lightly on the muzzle.

He heard Spook move closer.

What are you doing, Ron?

The room started to spin, making him sick. Ron lifted his head up, breathing through his nose, trying to fight the nausea. "Imagine if I actually did it?" he said. "Man, he would freak, using his precious shotgun for that. And without his permission!"

Stop it, Spook said.

Ron waved his hand in her direction. "It would be so easy."

He took a deep breath as he rested his head on the muzzle again. This time he kept his eyes open, to prevent the dizziness.

Ron swore. He saw that the barrel was smeared with his blood. It had run down the barrel and soaked into the carpet.

"Oh geez!" he said. "Look at this mess! Dad'll freak!"

He leaned the shotgun against the desk as he looked around. There was blood everywhere, even the papers on his father's desk were spattered with dark stains. Ron felt a bit panicky despite all the scotch he'd drunk. He grabbed his shirt and began to wipe the desk, tried to blot the papers. After a few tries he gave up and started to laugh.

"I've done it now!" he said. He sat back, knowing that Spook was watching him. "Better leave old dad a note. Tell him I'll clean it in the morning." He grabbed a clean sheet of letterhead with the name of his father's law firm embossed at the top. Ron took the Mont Blanc fountain pen from the desk set and began to scribble his note. After four words, he stopped, shaking his head.

"Who am I kidding?" he said. "What's the point in a note? He'll freak anyway!"

He placed the letterhead on top of the other papers and struggled to return the pen to its proper place. It took a few tries before he replaced the thick pen in its spot.

Ron pushed the chair back from the desk, forgetting about the shotgun still leaning against it, still loaded, hammers still cocked. As he turned away, the chair hit the shotgun and Ron saw it, finally remembering. He swore and reached for it, his alcohol muddled reflexes making him clumsy. The shotgun slid toward him, muzzle first. Ron tried to grab it by the breech, but his blood-slicked fingers slipped and his thumb caught inside the trigger guard.

Dad likes the pull light, less than five ounces.

Ron saw the barrel slip closer, felt his balance go with his thumb still in the guard.

Then he remembered the note on his father's desk, the four words he had written there.

"Sorry about the mess."

Something moved above him. Spook rushed forward, reaching out. She came closer, he saw a flash of blonde hair and a hand grabbing the barrel before his thumb made contact with the trigger. Then Spook leaned forward, pale and terrified, the shotgun slipping from her hands. It crashed onto the desk, bounced and then slid off, taking the blotter and all the items it held with it.

"You idiot!" Spook yelled. "You stupid idiot! What were you thinking?"

She sat on the carpet, stuck between the desk and the cabinets beneath the wet bar. She was shaking violently. Ron shook his head. His vision was blurry, but he saw that the girl wasn't Spook. She stood up and grabbed his arm, examining the deep gash.

"Jesus, you're a mess!" Eilean said. "Get up, Ron. I'm taking you to the hospital."

Chapter 17
Eilean

They sat at the far end of the hospital cafeteria, Eilean sipping coffee, Cathy staring at the glass of apple juice sitting on the table in front of her. There was a small pool of juice on the table and Cathy began to trace patterns in it with her straw. Ron was on Cathy's right, staring into space. His left arm was bandaged and slung tightly to his chest, wrist secured above his heart.

"To help stop the bleeding," the emergency nurse had told them hours before.

Their conversation hadn't exactly been riveting, but Eilean saw that Cathy appreciated the company. She was on some kind of medication, and seemed to fade in and out. Ron was still dazed by his close encounter with the shotgun.

Cathy's parents sat at a nearby table, drinking tea and not speaking. She had been admitted into the hospital for a twenty-four-hour watch. Ron's mother sat with them, looking uncomfortable. She clenched a wadded ball of tissue in her right hand and her eyes were red and puffy. Ron's father had left as soon as he was told Ron would be okay.

"You and I are going to have a long talk when you get home," were the only words Mr Freis said to Ron. His father had been nasty to everyone, but Eilean had seen him as he waited outside the ward. His hands had trembled as he tried to light a cigarette. Ron had slept on a stretcher near emergency, waking up an hour or so ago. He didn't look very refreshed, but at least he was sober.

Eilean glanced at the clock over the exit doors. It was just past six in the morning. She had gone nearly a whole day without sleep. She didn't think she would have a good sleep for a long, long time.

"I guess I'll have to get a new one," Cathy said. Hers was the only voice in the cafeteria. Eilean and Ron looked at her. It was the first time she had spoken in nearly an hour.

"A new what?" Eilean asked.

"Drawing pad. I lost mine up at the Gorge."

Eilean picked up her backpack, remembering. She opened it and took out the thick sketchbook.

"Here," she said. "I found it up on the trail."

Cathy took the sketchbook in both hands, hugging it tight to her chest the way a child held her favourite toy. She looked over at Eilean and smiled.

Eilean smiled back and the conversation lapsed again. She looked over at the entrance and saw someone familiar walk in. The only people to enter while they had been sitting here were a few patients and staff. She watched Sarah's father pour himself a coffee then wander near the table, without seeing who sat at it.

"Would you like to sit with us?" Eilean asked. He looked a little apprehensive, but sat anyway.

Man he looks tired, she thought.

"How's Debbie?" Eilean asked. Mr Spokes took a sip of his coffee before answering.

"The doctor gave her something to help her sleep. She's not taking this very well."

She nodded. He put down his coffee and looked at her.

"She didn't mean what she said before. She was just upset. We both were."

Eilean nodded again. There was nothing to say.

"If anyone is to blame," he said, "it's us, for not seeing this coming."

Eilean felt a catch in her throat. She leaned forward and put her hand over his.

"We'll get through this," she said. "Together."

He looked at her and smiled faintly

"How's Sarah doing?" Ron asked. Eilean was surprised at his directness. Mr Spokes looked at Ron, not recognizing him from yesterday afternoon. She saw that he was wondering what had happened to Ron's arm.

"This is Ron," Eilean said, explaining. "A friend of Sarah's from school."

Mr Spokes nodded.

"No change. The doctors say they have to wait. See if she wakes up on her own. They said her chances of recovery depend on how long the blood supply was cut from her brain."

"Can't they do scans or something?" Eilean asked.

He shook his head. "They said nothing shows up this early."

"She'll be okay," Cathy said. "Sarah's tough."

Sarah's father didn't look very convinced. "The doctors did say that if she wakes up in the first twenty-four-hours, it's a real good sign." He looked at his watch and smiled faintly. "About an hour or so to go."

They didn't discuss what would happen if she didn't wake up.

There was a bit more polite conversation before he excused himself, wanting to go back up to the ward to check on his wife and daughter. Eilean was glad to have heard something about Sarah's condition. Since she wasn't family, the nurses wouldn't allow her onto the ward.

"He doesn't look good, does he?" Cathy said, rather obviously. Eilean didn't respond. "I wonder how Jamie's family is."

Eilean had got up the courage to visit Jamie's family after Cathy had been taken to the hospital. Jamie's house was quite far from hers, but she needed the walk. She saw a few cars in the driveway, one of them with rental stickers on the bumper. Probably his brother and sister. They lived out east now.

She approached the front door and gently touched the oblong silver mezuzah attached to the right side of the door frame. Jamie had told her it contained a verse from the Old Testament. Eilean took a deep breath before ringing the doorbell. There was no response and she debated trying it again. Instead, she turned away, not sure what she would say anyway. She was halfway down the steps when the door opened and she heard a voice.

"Yes?"

Eilean turned and thought she saw Jamie holding the door open.

She blinked and looked again. This was an adult, taller, a little heavier than Jamie. They had the same olive skin, the same wavy hair and wire-framed glasses. She realized it was Josh, his brother.

"Sorry," she said. "I didn't want to bother you. I just wanted to see how your parents were."

She hadn't moved, still standing halfway down the steps.

"Are you a friend of Jamie's?"

"Yes. I'm Eilean. We've met a couple of times before."

"Yes, that's right." She saw he didn't really remember her. He shifted his weight and the door opened a little wider. Eilean saw a few people gathered in the living room. Jamie's sister held her mother, who was weeping uncontrollably. Eilean looked away.

"This isn't a good time," Josh said. "Perhaps you could come back when we sit Shiva."

Eilean nodded, not really understanding, and Josh started to close the door.

159

"Thanks for coming by," he said. She nodded again.

"Wait," he said as she turned away. "Is it true his girlfriend tried to kill herself, too?"

Eilean turned back, a little confused. Had Jamie told his family that Sarah was his girlfriend? Or was it Cathy?

"Yes," Eilean said. "She's in hospital."

Josh shook his head and swore. She had the feeling that it wasn't something he did often.

"What were they thinking?" he asked.

Eilean had no answer.

* * *

Eileen looked at the cafeteria clock again, restless.

"Let's go for a walk," she said. Cathy and Ron stood while Eilean cleared the table. Cathy told her parents what they were doing and they agreed wearily. Her mother warned her to stay inside the hospital.

The halls were silent as they wandered. Cathy shoved her hands in the pockets of her hospital robe and stared at everyone with the directness of a child. Somehow they ended up on the intensive care ward and the nurses didn't give them a second glance.

I guess we look like we belong in here, Eilean thought.

They walked slowly down the corridor. Many of the rooms they passed had their doors propped open. Most of them were silent, but they heard moans escaping from a few. In the centre of the ward was a small lounge and Eilean saw Sarah's father sitting on a worn leather couch. His wife lay next to him asleep, covered by a hand-quilted blanket. The television was on, but he stared off into space, a coffee cup forgotten in his hand.

They found Sarah's room two doors down. She lay motionless on the bed, and the only noise in the room came from the machines keeping her alive. Her pale blonde hair lay limp against the pillow. Her face was swollen and purple, a tube taped inside her mouth. The three of them stood there for few moments until it became too painful to stay. Ron was the first to turn away. Eilean felt tears sting, but she fought them. She saw that the distant look had returned to Cathy's eyes. Ron didn't look much more alert. Eilean stopped at the nurse's station.

"Can you give me an update on Sarah Spokes?"

The nurse looked at her quizzically for a moment, and then glanced at the others. She checked a file.

"No change. She's still listed as serious but stable. Are you family?"

Eilean looked at her motley crew before answering. "Yes."

"I'm sorry," the nurse said.

"Is there any chance of her waking up?" Ron asked. The nurse hesitated before answering.

"It would be best for you to discuss that with the doctors."

Eilean thanked her and turned away, leading Cathy.

"I don't think I want to go back," Cathy said. "To the Gorge."

It was something Cathy had done all night, making these statements out of the blue.

"It was my favourite place."

"I know," Eilean said.

Beside them, Ron sighed deeply, shuddering, trying to hold back his tears. Eilean touched his good arm gently.

"What is it?"

"You really think there's a chance she'll make it?"

"I don't know," Eilean replied. Deep down, she didn't think so. The only thing keeping Sarah alive was the machines.

"You know what's sad?" Cathy said. Eilean shook her head, thinking: Yes I do, but where to begin?

"Sarah wanted to go out in style. She told me she hoped she could hang around afterwards, to see everyone's reaction."

"Yeah, that sounds like Sarah," Eilean said.

"Look at her now," Ron said. "Just lying there. Just hanging on. Not real dramatic, is it?" They walked on.

"You never talk about your mom," Cathy said. Eileen guessed that the medication she was on was making Cathy's brain work in strange ways. "Would you tell me about her one day?"

"Maybe," she said. "One day." One day when the sadness wasn't so overwhelming, when she could think of Jamie and Sarah without falling to pieces. She had decided she would talk with her dad first. They had ignored her mom's death too long. It was time to talk.

They had reached the elevators at the end of the hall. Eilean saw the three of them reflected on the polished metal of the doors. Ron had his good hand to his mouth, scratching, covering a yawn. Cathy was rubbing her eyes.

We look like the Evil Monkeys.

Eilean smiled, remembering the three monkeys she'd see in cartoons, one covering his eyes, one his ears, the other his mouth. When she was small she called them the Evil Monkeys.

We're not the Evil Monkeys, though, Eilean thought. We have our own saying: See no suicide, hear no suicide, speak no suicide. Maybe we should start a band, call ourselves the Suicide Monkeys.

The elevator doors opened and they stepped inside. Cathy fiddled with the plastic ID bracelet on her right wrist.

"Serious but stable," Cathy said, not looking up. Eilean glanced over at her, saw a distant smile on her friend's face.

"Serious but stable," Eilean said. "Sounds like all of us."

AGMV Marquis

MEMBER OF SCABRINI MEDIA

Quebec, Canada
2003